UNLOCKING DREAMS (SPECIAL FORCES: OPERATION ALPHA)

A FLIPPING LOVE STORY, BOOK 1

LINZI BAXTER

Dear Readers,

Welcome to the Special Forces: Operation Alpha Fan-Fiction world!

If you are new to this amazing world, in a nutshell the author wrote a story using one or more of my characters in it. Sometimes that character has a major role in the story, and other times they are only mentioned briefly. This is perfectly legal and allowable because they are going through Aces Press to publish the story.

This book is entirely the work of the author who wrote it. While I might have assisted with brainstorming and other ideas about which of my characters to use, I didn't have any part in the process or writing or editing the story.

I'm proud and excited that so many authors loved my characters enough that they wanted to write them into their own story. Thank you for supporting them, and me!

READ ON!

Xoxo

Susan Stoker

ABOUT THE BOOK

A dream house. A dream man. And a nightmare that could destroy everything.

Six years after Isabella Harper's unscrupulous boss destroyed her real estate career, her house-flipping business is on the brink of success—or it would be, if her main competition, sexy ex-SEAL Ian Parker, wasn't outbidding her on every promising flip in town.

Finally, she lands a neglected Victorian home that will fix her ruined reputation. Except a persistent vandal threatens to derail her tight schedule and even tighter budget. Plus, Ian inexplicably starts showing up, offering to help. And making her heart hammer with desire.

It's not just profits that drives Ian to keep plenty of flippable houses his reno pipeline. Working himself to exhaustion keeps his deployment nightmares at bay. But letting Bella win that house is worth the smile she aims at him...and now he can't get enough of it. Or her.

As they work side by side, Ian dares to hope he's

close to bidding his heart goodbye. But when Bella suddenly disappears, his nightmare takes on a new face. Hers…if he doesn't reach her in time to save her from a threat no one saw coming.

ACKNOWLEDGMENTS

I would like to express my gratitude to the many people who saw me through this book. My editor, who did an amazing job and worked hard to help me craft a better story. Cassy, for doing an astounding job with the cover art. My husband and family, for always being there to support me. This book couldn't have happened without Susan Stoker allowing me to write in her world!

Thank you to all you amazing readers who are going on this journey alongside me. I hope *Unlocking Dreams* is all that you hoped for and more!

DEDICATION

Jean and Michelle for always listening to my ideas.

CHAPTER 1

Isabella Harper analyzed the growing crowd around her. She recognized most of the bidders gathered at the bottom of the Bexar County Courthouse steps. That day, Bexar County would auction off one house. Isabella was determined to win the bid—she wouldn't let another house slip from her grasp. She needed this house to propel her new real estate company, Bella Estates.

She gritted her teeth in frustration when she spotted Ian Parker, her biggest competitor at the auction. The ex-Navy SEAL seemed to have an endless bank account. Even though he angered her by buying up all the available houses, it was hard to peel her eyes away from his body. He towered over her five-foot-two, vertically challenged height. His muscles strained against his black T-shirt. Her gaze slowly worked its way up his body until her eyes reached his. He had a knowing smirk.

No matter how sexy the competition was, she needed to concentrate on the auction.

Six months earlier, everything Bella had worked for had tumbled down around her. She was with the top real estate investor in San Antonio, Alton Ainsworth. He'd shown her how to get the best deals, and she'd become his apprentice. He included Bella when he negotiated new deals. When she wasn't in the office, learning from her mentor, she was at a job site. Mr. Ainsworth planned to retire and hand the business over to Bella.

The only part of the business he hadn't shown her was the company's books. She constantly asked about the accounting side of the business, and Mr. Ainsworth came up with a different excuse each time. Bella understood why when the FBI showed up one Tuesday morning and seized the office's computers. She sat in her office in the executive wing of Ainsworth Real Estate. The glass wall gave her a front-row view of the FBI agents as they escorted her boss out of the building in handcuffs.

The FBI interviewed everyone in the office, and the employees of Ainsworth Real Estate were cleared, but Mr. Ainsworth got sentenced to thirty years in jail for embezzlement and wire fraud. Bella was shocked that she hadn't seen what her mentor had done. Because she'd been his second-in-command, her name had been tarnished in the real estate business.

After the FBI cleared her, she decided to flip her first house with what little savings she had. If she could get her hands on the house on auction that day, it would set her up for the rest of the year. Bella planned to try to buy it for less than $200,000. She would make a $100,000 profit when she sold the house. Ian was the only person in the way of her dream.

The double doors to the courthouse swung open. Benny, the county auctioneer, walked down the stairs. He was in his late fifties. His white button-down shirt strained against his beer belly. The top of his head was beaded with sweat from the Texas sun.

Bella glanced to where Ian Parker stood. Next to him was an equally sexy man, but something about Ian held her attention. She took the extra second to memorize his features while he spoke to his friend. He must have felt her gaze because he looked up and winked. His cocky demeanor made her want to win the bid even more.

Benny cleared his throat. "We have one house up for auction today: 103 Fairlane Road. The lender has set the opening bid at one hundred fifty thousand dollars. The bidding will start in five-thousand-dollar increments. Okay, the auction's on. What would you give for it? The bid is one hundred fifty thousand. Now, give a hundred fifty-five."

The Lang brothers bid $155. They normally went after duplexes, so it surprised her to see them at the auction.

"Now, will you give one sixty-five? Do I have one sixty… going once… going twi—"

Ian shouted, "One seventy."

Before the auctioneer had time to confirm the bid, a man standing behind Ian said, "Two hundred." He wore a blue hoody. Bella had never seen him before.

The crowd groaned. The newcomer's bid hike caused a few of the locals to leave. The Lang brothers were the first to head toward the parking garage.

"One seventy… now two hundred… do I have two hundred five? Two hundred five… going once… going twice…"

Ian nodded, taking the bid.

Bella needed this house. It was time to make her

move. "Two ten."

"I have two ten. Anyone else give two fifteen...? Would you give two fifteen?"

The man with the blue hoody motioned for the two fifteen bid.

The bidding war made Bella's adrenaline spike. She shouted, "Two twenty-five."

Blue-hoody man said something she couldn't hear and stormed off toward the parking lot. Ian watched Bella. She hoped with all her heart that he would let her have this house. He'd taken the last six houses that were up for auction.

In the background, the auctioneer continued his chant. "...Bids at two hundred twenty-five dollars... do I hear two thirty? Would you go for two thirty?"

Bella shut her eyes and hoped all the bidders would keep their traps closed. When the auction hit $200,000, a majority of the bidders left. They wouldn't stand out in the Texas heat any longer than necessary. Most of them had large renovation crews and needed to have a certain price to make a profit. Bella planned to do most of the work herself. This would be her ticket back into the real estate world. She would fix her name. She vowed to never work with another company again. Alton Ainsworth had burned her too badly.

Bella had no clue about how bad the Victorian home was inside, but she hoped she could salvage most of it so she could make a profit. The house had great curb appeal. The outside didn't concern her—the inside was what she was nervous about.

She heard Benny shout, "Going once… going twice… going thrice. Sold to this lady."

Her dream had come true. Ian's eyes were narrowed in her direction. She couldn't figure out what he wanted, but at the moment, she didn't care. The house was hers. This called for a celebration. She sent her friend Ava a text to see if she could meet her at the diner across the street.

Bella paid for the house with a cashier's check and filled out paperwork. An hour later, she walked out of the courthouse, the new owner of a Victorian house.

* * *

"Was he there?" Ava asked Bella.

"Who?"

Bella leaned back in the booth at Joe's Diner and held back her smile. Ava had become one of her closest friends. Mr. Ainsworth had used the company Ava worked for to sell homes. After a few meetings, they'd become friends. After the FBI arrested Bella's boss, Ava was the only person in the real estate industry to call and ask how she was. Ava was tall and slender, and she loved spending time at home with her fiancé. Like her, Bella loved to spend time at home, but with a book, not a boyfriend.

"You know who I'm talking about. The former Navy SEAL who buys all the houses from under you. Each time you complain about him, you get a far-off look in your eyes."

"He was there," Bella grumbled. She wouldn't deny that she fantasized about the man. "Ian showed up with one of his friends and bid the house up, but not as high as he normally does. It would be so much easier to hate the man if he wasn't so damn hot."

"Instead of spending hours fantasizing about him, why don't you ask him out? Can you imagine the team you would make or the mini-humans you could produce? They would have your eye for design and his endless pocketbook."

Bella choked on her water. After Ava had fallen head over heels in love with her hunky FBI Agent, Ethan Riker, she'd tried to set Bella up on a few blind dates. Bella was able to dodge each of them. Now Ava wanted her to hook up with the enemy.

"Ava, I asked you to lunch to celebrate my new

project. I don't have time for a man in my life. I'm still in the process of picking up the pieces from six months ago. I want to talk about the house."

"Fine. When are you going to start on the house?" Ava asked before she bit into her burger.

Bella pulled the keys out and jingled them. "They gave me the keys at the auction. I plan to head over to the house after our lunch. The lumberyard will be my next stop. The house needs to be back on the market in three weeks."

Ava's phone buzzed with a new message. When she glanced down at it, her eyes twinkled with love, and Bella knew her fiancé had texted her. Ava replied to the message and put her phone back in her pocket. "Three weeks is a tight schedule. Are you hiring subs to help you hit the timeline?"

Bella sighed. "I'm hiring a couple of contractors, but I plan to do most of the work myself. This is my only job for the next three weeks. If I spend every waking hour at the site, I should be able to finish in three weeks."

"I know I won't be able to talk you out of your crazy schedule. How about I come over on Sunday and help for a few hours?" Ava held up her hand and stopped Bella from interrupting. "Ethan has to work this weekend, and I don't have any showings on

Sunday. I hate sitting at home alone, so let me help you."

"I would love the help." Bella took a sip of water. "But please don't feel you have to."

"I want to help. Then you can flip the house quickly and see your sexy SEAL." Ava wagged her eyebrows.

Bella shook her head. Ava wouldn't drop it until she dated someone. She hadn't tried since the incident with her boss. The FBI had cleared her name, but not before the media had dragged it through the mud along with her mentor's. High-powered people who were angry at her ex-boss shifted their anger to her when they could no longer reach him. She was scared to date again.

"Stop thinking about your old boss." Ava could always read her mind.

"It's hard. He cheated so many people out of money. How did I not see this?"

"How long was he in business?"

They'd had this argument before. "Thirty years."

Ava pointed at her. "He did millions in transactions. You aren't the only person he fooled. Let it be in the past, and move forward."

"You're right." Bella sighed.

Ava's phone buzzed. "I have a meeting with a new

client in a half hour. I'll see you on Sunday. Do you need me to bring anything?"

"Nope. Come hungry. I'll have lunch for us."

"Can't wait."

Bella let out a laugh. "You can't wait to do manual labor?"

"I always see the houses once they're complete. It will be fun to be part of the process of fixing the house."

Bella and Ava exited the booth and hugged. "Thank you for helping me," Bella said. "I swear I will give you an easy job."

"I offered to help, so don't give me busy work." Ava pulled her purse strap over her shoulder.

Bella held up her hands. "I promise: no busy work."

"Good."

Outside the diner, they hugged again. "See you Sunday," Bella said. "If something comes up, please don't worry about canceling."

"I'll be there. Be careful."

"Always am. Bye."

Excitement coursed through Bella's veins the closer she got to her new Victorian home. She hoped she'd made the right decision. This flip could make or break her future.

CHAPTER 2

Ian Parker parked in front of the yellow Victorian home and turned off his engine. He'd wanted this house—it would have been a great flip. The curb appeal alone was enough to sell the house. The white wrap-around balcony accented the yellow siding. A pebbled sidewalk led up to the teal steps. The home was just under three thousand square feet. It would have been a nice addition to the houses he'd already flipped.

The neighborhood was quaint and quiet and screamed old money. He was surprised that the house had sold for so low a price. Isabella would get a nice profit off the flip.

Cole Walker, his business partner, had been surprised when Ian had stopped bidding on the house, but Ian couldn't help but want to give Bella the bid. Her husky voice had gone straight to his groin. She'd worn a navy-blue suit that accented her curves. The pants bunched at the bottom even with her wearing high heels. Bella had to be almost a foot shorter than his six-foot-four frame. After making the bid of $225,000, she closed her eyes and bit her lip, and he knew she needed this house. People in the crowd whispered about her old boss. They all believed she'd been in on his scheme. Ian never paid close attention to the gossip, but something had tugged at his heartstrings, and he let her have the house. Her eyes had lit up with joy when the auctioneer said, "Sold."

Losing one house would not send Ian into a downward spiral. He'd sent Cole out to find him another one. Cole and Ian had met in the Navy. They'd both been part of SEAL Team Five and stationed in Korea. Ian was medically discharged, and Cole left a few months later when he had the option to leave or reenlist. After that, they used their savings and flipped houses. Cole did it for the money. Ian did it to help with his PTSD. The demolition of the houses helped wear him down so that he could sleep at night without having nightmares.

A shadow along the side of the house snapped

Ian out of his thoughts. It looked like someone in a black hooded sweatshirt. Isabella's Mini Cooper sat in the driveway, and he could see her working through the front picture window.

Ian exited his F-150 pickup and decided to see who was walking around the side of the house. Ian's boots crunched on the pebbled walkway. At the side of the house, a slender person held a spray can and was painting the wall.

"What are you doing?" Ian growled.

The person dropped the can and took off toward the backyard. Ian cursed under his breath and chased after him. When Ian rounded the back of the house, the perp jumped into a red Honda and squealed out of the back neighbor's driveway. Ian squinted to see the license plate. He didn't have his glasses on, so the numbers were a blur.

"Fuck." He walked back to the scene of the crime. The person had spray-painted, "Get out Bitch."

When he stomped back to the front of the house, Isabella peeked her head out the window. Her crystal-blue eyes widened when they landed on him. He couldn't help but wink. It made her blush.

The white door to the Victorian home swung open, and Isabella stormed out onto the wrap-around porch. She stopped at the top of the stairs and placed her hands on her hips. "What are you doing here, Mr. Parker?"

Damn, she was hot when she was angry.

"I wanted to see inside the house." That was partially true.

"Why?"

"How about we table that discussion for a second? When I pulled up to the house, I caught someone going around the side. I went to see what was going on, and I caught someone vandalizing your house."

"Fuck. Again," Isabella mumbled.

He almost didn't hear what she'd said, but the word *again* set off alarm bells. Before he had time to ask, she stormed down the stairs and headed to the side of the house. Ian followed behind her. When her eyes landed on the vandalized wall, he could see a sheen in them before she blinked. She turned and headed back toward the front of the house.

"I'm going to call the cops," Ian said. They needed to file a report.

"No, it's probably some kid." Isabella let out a sigh and filled a pail with water and soap. "I'll clean it up again. They'll get sick of doing this soon."

"What do you mean 'again'? Someone has spray-painted the house more than once?"

"They spray-painted on the first day and broke a window yesterday. Move, so I can get this cleaned off." Isabella tried to push her way around him.

"Stop, Isabella."

"Bella."

He cocked his head.

Isabella let out a sigh. "I go by Bella. Please don't call me Isabella."

"Okay, Bella. We need to call the cops. After they take your report, I'll help you clean this up."

For a second, Ian thought she would argue with him again. Instead, she turned on her heel and headed toward the front door. He couldn't pry his eyes from her hips as they swayed with each step. Her tight black yoga pants accented her curves.

He followed her into the house. It took a second for his eyes to adjust to the dim light inside the Victorian home. While Bella paced back and forth, talking to dispatch, Ian wandered over to the living room. The fireplace was a work of art. He ran his hands over the engraved wood. It was pure craftsmanship. He kneeled to examine the inside. Someone had filled it in. Ian was so engaged in wondering how he could make the fireplace work again that he didn't hear Bella walk up behind him until she placed a dainty hand on his shoulder.

"It's a shame someone would seal up a piece of art," she said.

"I don't think it would be too hard to revert it." He pointed to the bricks that lined the back of the chimney. "Once you remove those bricks, you'll be able to tell why they closed it up. Many people don't want to deal with the upkeep of chimneys and decide it's easier to close them."

When she didn't answer right away, he looked over his shoulder. She had her lip between her teeth. "I'll take your advice into account."

He could tell she had no plan to take his advice. It wasn't his place to push her. This was her flip, not his.

"Are the cops on the way?"

"Yes. You don't have to stay." She reached for her paintbrush. "I don't think they'll be here for another hour."

He took a step forward, waiting until she turned before he spoke. "I already told you I would help you clean the side of the house. Why don't you show me the rest of the house? Then I can help you paint if you have another roller."

"You really don't have to stay."

Ian didn't see the point in replying. He headed for the grand staircase. When he gripped the railing, it jiggled. He heard Isabella's footsteps behind him. On each step up, the stairs creaked under his weight. He made a mental note of all the things that needed repairing.

When he turned right down the hall, Bella said, "Mr. Parker, come this way." She turned the other direction.

He wouldn't argue. Ian followed her and watched the sway of her hips. Since he'd seen Isabella in her yoga pants, his dick had been hard.

"This is my favorite room." Isabella opened the door to the master bedroom.

Any buyer would fall in love with the room. It had the original wood floors and—as with downstairs—a masterpiece of a fireplace, though this one was in working order. Floor-to-ceiling windows lined the side of the room, showing a view of the lake.

He nodded. "You won't have any trouble selling this house. When do you plan to put it on the market?"

Isabella let out a sigh and ran her hand through her hair. "My goal is a three-week flip." Before he could tell her that was a crazy timeline, she held up her hand. "I know it's a short timeline. This is my only project going on. If only the vandalizing would stop."

"Why are you rushing?"

"I don't have money to throw around," she snapped.

Ian had suspected she was short on money. At the auctions, when she lost a bid, she would look so defeated. And because of her ties to Mr. Ainsworth, no one would lend her money. Ian also knew her pride was too high, and she would turn down any money he offered. He had some spare time to help her, and he could keep his eye on her. He needed to work to protect her house from being vandalized.

He ignored her snap. "Let's head downstairs, and I'll help you paint."

For ten minutes, they worked without speaking. It was easy to work next to her.

Isabella broke the silence. "So… why are you here?"

"I wanted to see the inside house." *And you,* he thought.

"I'm surprised you didn't bid me up more on this house. You seem to have bought every house on the auction block in the past three months."

Ian had no plan to tell her the real reason he'd bought so many houses. Isabella didn't need to know he suffered from PTSD, and working on the flips to the point at which his body would tire out was the only way he could sleep at night.

Eight years earlier, SEAL Team Five had been on a mission to North Korea to bring back information on a missing SEAL team the CIA had uncovered. The information was false, according to a CIA mole in North Korea. When his team arrived to save the missing SEAL team, the North Koreans ambushed them. They tortured his team for five days. It had felt like a year. He and Cole were the only two to survive the torture. Later, information came out that the CIA mole had flipped sides and had been helping North Korea.

The ring of the doorbell saved Ian from answering Isabella's question.

CHAPTER 3

Bella didn't understand why talking about Ian's bidding habits brought a storm of emotions across his face. When the doorbell rang, she still wanted to know why the topic upset him. She couldn't imagine why he wouldn't be happy about all the good deals he'd gotten over the past few months.

She reached for the door. On the other side stood a police officer around six-two—a couple inches shorter than Ian. The man had short dark brown hair. She couldn't see his eyes behind the dark glasses.

"Are you Ms. Harper?" the officer asked.

She opened the door wider for the officer to come in. "Yes, and your name is…?"

Before he could reply, Ian said, "Hey, Max."

The two men reached out their hands to do a manly handshake-hug. Bella's ovaries were in overdrive, but she needed to get the vandalism noted and get back to work even though she had two hot men in her house.

The three gathered around the kitchen counter. "Now, Ms. Harper, my name is Officer Max Anders. Can you please tell me what happened?

"Please call me Bella." She let out a sigh. "When I showed up after the auction, someone had spray-painted 'Leave, bitch' across the garage. I figured they were targeting the previous owners. Yesterday, when I arrived, someone had busted a window in the back of the house." She had covered the broken window with plywood. In two days, a window installer was scheduled to fix it. "Then today, someone painted on the side of the house again. Officer, I'm sorry to bother you. I think they don't know the house has a new owner."

Ian and the officer gave each other a look she didn't understand. "How long has the house been empty?" Anders asked.

She had no clue.

Ian said, "The previous family moved out two

years ago. Their oldest daughter went missing. The family couldn't live in the house anymore because it reminded them of their daughter. They bought the house during the housing boom. It's been empty for two years. I don't think they're targeting the previous owners."

How the hell did that man know so much about the house? She'd never looked into why the house was empty, only how much she could get for it. *Damn.* The man was sexy and smart. The more he was around, the more she wanted to spend time with him.

"How do you know so much about the previous owners?" she asked.

Ian shrugged. "I research all houses I might buy."

"So this means the person is after you," Officer Anders said. "Is there anyone you've upset or someone who might be mad at you?"

Her enemy list was a mile long. Thanks to her ex-boss, everyone in the San Antonio real estate business was her enemy. People she'd never even talked to hated her. Why wouldn't people believe she had nothing to do with what her boss had done?

"I might have a few people in the real estate business who don't like me," she said.

The officer took notes. It was nice to know he

took the situation seriously. She hadn't reported the issue earlier because she hadn't wanted to waste their time.

He looked up from his notepad. "Could you give me a list of people you think would come after you?"

"How about everyone in real estate?"

When Officer Anders looked confused, Ian explained, "Isabella was Mr. Ainsworth's number two."

He let out a whistle. "Ms. Harper, you need to add cameras, and you need to make sure you aren't here alone."

"Thank you for the recommendations," Bella said. How would she pay for cameras and a bodyguard? She had one mission: to flip the house and make a profit so she could fund her next flip. One option would be to spend her time at the house instead of going home each night. That way, she would also get more work done on the house.

Officer Anders put his notepad in his pocket and asked to see the vandalism. The paint on the side of the house had dried. She wouldn't be able to scrub it off. *Fuck.* She would have to repaint the side of the house. Officer Anders bent down and took pictures of the spray can then pulled out an evidence bag from his back pocket and put the can in it. He sealed the top of the bag with red tape.

Over the next few minutes, he took pictures of the house and documented the route the perp had taken. Bella already knew there wasn't enough evidence to find whoever had done this, but with a police report filed, if the person came back, the police could charge them for the previous incidents.

Officer Anders left in his patrol car. Bella didn't want the neighbors to complain about the graffiti on the side of the house, so she grabbed a roller and the paint. She expected Ian to leave with Officer Anders. Instead, he grabbed another roller and helped her paint the side of the house. They worked in silence, but her body hummed with how close he was to her. Every so often, her elbow would brush against him.

After cleaning up the rollers, Ian walked her to the front door. For the first time, he seemed nervous. "Isabe—"

"Please call me Bella."

"Bella, will you have dinner with me Friday night?"

The question shocked her. Ian was handsome and successful. What would he want with her? It had been years since she'd been on a date. When she was working for Mr. Ainsworth, she focused on her career. For the past six months, she'd tried to resurrect her career. But she would be dumb not to say yes to the sexy, hot man who stood at her doorstep.

"Yes," she squeaked out.

He pulled his phone from his pocket. "Can I have your number? I'll text you closer to Friday so we can make plans."

She rambled off her digits, and she could hear her phone ring from inside the house. Excitement coursed through her veins. Too bad Friday was four days away.

He leaned in and wrapped his arms around her. She leaned into him and enjoyed the feel of his hard muscles. Ian smelled of sawdust and outdoors. The hug ended too soon.

"Go inside, and lock the door. If you see anything else, call me right away. Don't forget what Officer Anders said: get cameras, and make sure your contractor is here with you at all times."

Bella didn't plan to tell him she didn't have a contractor. She would do the work herself. She didn't plan on getting cameras either.

She nodded and walked inside. Once the deadbolt clicked, she heard his steps leave the front porch. She didn't even have time to process the morning when her cell phone rang from the other room.

She picked up the phone and saw that the caller was Ava. "You won't believe who just left my house," Bella told her.

Ava didn't miss a beat. "I bet it was a hunky ex-SEAL you drool over all the time."

"How did you know?"

It was a stupid question. Bella didn't have many friends, and the only person who would surprise her was Ian.

"That's the only person who rattles your solid exterior," Ava said. "But he puts you on edge in a good way. Did he ask you out?"

Bella was still in shock from being asked out. "Yes. I can't believe he asked me out. He showed up to see the house and then scared away the person who vandalized it." She heard Ava inhale on the other end of the phone. "After the officer left the house, Ian helped me clean up and asked me out Friday night."

"Hold on. Someone vandalized your new house?"

"It's fine. Ian made me call the cops, and we put a police report in. Officer Anders was really nice and documented everything."

"Officer Max Anders?" Ava asked.

"Yeah, why?"

"If you'd come over to the house last night like I asked, you would have met him. He is one of Ethan's close friends. I know he did a good job. What I don't understand is why you didn't tell me yesterday when I was helping you. Is that why the back window is boarded up? I figured that had been done when the house sat empty."

Ava had shown up Sunday morning and helped her paint. Bella hadn't told her friend about the issues with vandalism because she didn't want to worry her. Before Ava left at noon, she invited Bella to come over for a barbeque. Bella had planned to go, but her body had ached from the four straight days of hard labor, so she'd gone to bed instead

"I thought it was someone going after the previous owners, so I didn't want to bother the police, but whoever it is knows it's me."

"You need to be safe," Ava said.

She needed to keep the house safe from whoever this person was. "I'm staying at the house," Bella said.

"I'm not sure that's a good idea."

"Ian left me his number. I'll call him if I need help."

"I still think you need to be more careful."

Bella loved how her friend worried about her.

But she would do this flip on her own. She reached for the roller. "Enough about me. How are you?"

"I originally called to make you feel guilty for not showing up yesterday and ask if you wanted to come out with everyone Friday. Since you clearly have plans for Friday, you have a pass, but you need to call me on Sunday and give me all the details."

"It's just dinner," Bella warned. "I know you want me to be happy like you, but don't get your hopes up. He's out of my league."

"You are beautiful. No one is out of your league."

There was no point in arguing with her. "Okay," Bella said. "I promise to call you on Sunday and let you know how it goes."

"I'm holding you to that. Are you sure you're safe in that house by yourself?"

"It's simple vandalism. It's not like an ax murderer showed up to the house or someone sliced my tires. It's windows and some paint. I'm fine."

"Okay. Don't forget to call."

"Talk to you Sunday," Bella said. "Bye."

Bella painted the living room after she got off the phone with Ava. She hadn't realized how late it was until she heard her phone beep. It was close to ten o'clock, but what sent her heart rate up was the text from Ian: *Good night, Bella. Call if you need anything.*

Her fingers trembled as she texted back: *Good night.*

She tossed and turned all night with images of Ian. When he'd given her a hug goodbye, her body had buzzed. She could imagine what it would be like to have her legs wrapped around his body.

CHAPTER 4

Four days had passed since Ian had left Bella's house. Deep down, he knew someone dangerous was after her. She seemed to not take her safety seriously. He found himself driving by her house a few times a day. Ian had become a stalker. He told himself it was to make sure she was okay, but he longed to see a glimpse of her.

Ian's new nightmares had replaced his old ones. They terrified him to the bone. For the last four nights, he'd dreamed he would find Bella's dead body. Bella would cry out for him, and he wouldn't get there in time. Each time he found her, blood oozed from the knife wounds in her abdomen. The dream felt so real that he would wake up with the copper taste of blood in his mouth.

Ian didn't hear Cole walk up until he was right behind him. "Hey, man, you look like shit. Are the nightmares back?"

He hadn't told his best friend about his impromptu stop at Bella's house or the constant drive-bys. He didn't know if Cole would be mad that he associated with her. Ian and Cole had never discussed Bella's past up until a week earlier, when she'd become the competition. Technically, she still was his competition, but he wanted to work with her.

Cole had grown up extremely privileged. His dad was the governor of Texas. His family also owned a large oil field. When Cole turned eighteen, he joined the military instead of continuing with the family legacy like his two older brothers. In the Walker family, there were two options: work for Walker Oil or start a career in politics. Cole wanted to help his country, so instead, he'd joined the military, and his family had disowned him.

Over the years, Cole had opened up about how his dad was corrupt politician, taking money under the table in order to get bills passed. He also felt his family was laundering money through Walker Oil. There wasn't enough evidence to prove his assumptions, but Cole had no tolerance for people who were corrupt or could be corrupted.

"Yes, and no," Ian said. "I stopped by Bella's flip the other day. I wanted to see the house. That place is a dream flip. When I arrived, someone was vandalizing the outside of the house. It wasn't the first time she had issues since she bought the place. I no longer dream about North Korea—Bella's dead body plagues me at night."

Cole was quiet for a few good seconds. "You like her." It was a statement, not a question.

"Yes."

Cole leaned against the new granite countertops. The two men stood in the kitchen of their latest flip. They would list it on Sunday. Cole and Ian had closed on a new property the previous day. Ian would start the new project on Monday.

"This house is practically done. You don't need to micromanage the decorators. Go home." Cole had a far-off look in his eyes.

Ian grabbed the white rag and wiped down the countertop. "If I go home and fall asleep, the dream comes back. If I stay here and work, it will take my mind off the dreams. And don't you think we should talk about the elephant in the room?"

Cole peered around the room. "I don't see an elephant."

Ian let out a chuckle. "You know what the fuck I'm talking about: Bella. She's a competitor, and there's her past. I don't want to upset you."

Cole narrowed his eyes at Ian. "I have no issue with Bella. She is nothing like my family. If she makes you happy, go for it. You also know we have contacts you could use to help protect her. Why don't you call Tex and see what he can dig up on why someone is after her?"

"We both know why someone is after her: she's paying for her boss's mistakes. You're right—I should've called Tex when everything started."

The Navy had used Tex when the two men were captured in North Korea. Cole and Ian owed him their lives. Ian had been hours away from dying when SEAL Team Six, led by Wolf, saved them. Tex was able to use his magical computer skills to feed Wolf and his team their exact location. Tex had been a Navy SEAL until an injury in the line of duty. He'd lost a leg. After that, he spent his days on the computer. Ian didn't know how he did it, but Tex could find anyone with his computer. Ian could barely turn a computer on.

He'd heard that Tex had helped Wolf's team out

when his now-wife Caroline was kidnapped and almost killed, but Tex had already done so much for him. He'd saved Ian's life, and now Ian was about to ask for another favor. What would happen if the vandalism turned out to be nothing, and he took Tex's time away from his current mission?

"Call him," Cole said. "I'll check out a couple of listings hitting the market in the next few days. If any of them are good, I'll send you pictures so you can let me know what you think."

Ian didn't take Cole's advice to head home and take a nap. He knew if he left, he would drive past Bella's house like the stalker he was. So instead, he worked in the master bedroom and hung a ceiling fan and touched up the paint on the wall. This house would land them a $200,000 profit. Ian did most of the work inside the house while Cole drove from neighborhood to neighborhood and looked for run-down houses and would make offers before the owners listed the houses on the open market. That was where they would make the best deals.

Everything in the colonial house Ian was working on was brand new, except the foundation. Ian and his team had stripped it down to the bare walls and rebuilt it. The view from the master bedroom would sell the house. The floor-to-ceiling windows he'd installed gave an uninterrupted view of the lake in the backyard. He could see his crew putting the last few boards on the boat ramp.

His phone vibrated in his pants pocket. Ian peeled his eyes from the dock to answer his phone. "Unknown caller" flashed across the screen. Ian swiped across the phone, hoping it wasn't a salesperson. He didn't want to go on vacation no matter how many times they said he'd won.

"Aqua." Tex's deep voice came through the phone. How had he known Ian was thinking about calling him?

"I don't go by that anymore, Tex. It's just Ian." Ian felt he didn't deserve his military nickname. He'd let down his team when they were captured because he'd led them into the ambush. The Purple Heart buried in the bottom drawer made him feel ashamed. He didn't deserve the recognition when most of his team had died.

"You never lose your call name. If it weren't for you, Cole would be dead, and the military wouldn't have gotten the intel you stole. Do you understand that with that intel, Wolf's team was able to save a hundred women from being sold on the black market?"

It didn't matter how many people he saved. He'd

sacrificed his team to get that information. He should have worked to find another way.

"I know you didn't call to talk about past missions," Ian said. "What's going on?"

"Cole called a little while ago and said you needed help. He didn't think you would call me."

Ian wanted to kill his best friend for going behind his back. He still didn't know if he wanted to bother Tex with Bella's problem. Hell, he hadn't wanted to call Tex because he was still ashamed of what had happened to his team. No matter how many times people said it wasn't his fault, he couldn't get past the screams of his teammates.

"Tex, I know you work for every branch of the military. I didn't want to bother you with this. I can find a private investigator to help, or the local police can take care of this."

"First of all, I'm never too busy to help you. You call me the second you ever need anything. I don't care if you think it's nothing. Secondly, I've hired someone to help me, and if I can't get it done, she can. Beth is almost as good as I am—she thinks she's better. So tell me what's going on." Tex's voice had a sharp edge to it. Ian had upset him by not calling. Once again, Ian disappointed a person who meant a lot to him.

Tex was right that Ian needed information on who was after Bella. "I don't know much about her besides her name, Isabella Harper. Her last employer, Mr. Ainsworth, stole millions, and she was his apprentice. The FBI cleared Bella of all wrongdoing, but individuals who were screwed over think she knew more."

Tex whistled. "I watched part of the case. Isabella could have hundreds of people after her. I'll pull the police records and start the dig. I recommend installing cameras on the house she's flipping. Send me the IP address of the cameras, and I can help monitor them. And, Aqua, never hesitate to call me again."

"I won't."

"Cole also mentioned you still had nightmares. Have you spoken to anyone? You need to talk to someone, or they'll get worse."

Now Ian really planned to kill his best friend. "After the next house, I'll look into talking to someone. For right now, I don't want to talk about it. Can you send me the info you get on Bella?"

The line was quiet for a few minutes. Ian didn't know whether Tex would drop the issue of his nightmares or not. When Tex finally replied, Ian let out the breath he'd been holding. "I'll send you what

I can find. I'm also sending the information on a good group you can go to in the Fort Worth area."

"Take care, Tex."

Ian spent the next six hours with his team, finishing the last touches on the house. This was the thirtieth flip that Cole and Ian had completed. Ian didn't need the money, so everything he made, he stuck in a savings account for the day when he would have a family to support.

He locked the front door on his way out and smiled at his accomplishment. Now they would have a long weekend off before starting the next house on Monday. His team was going to the bar to celebrate being done a day early and had invited Ian along. Most times, he had a beer with the team, but he needed to go home and sleep. The following day, he would get to see Bella.

Ian couldn't stop himself—on his way home, he drove by Bella's house. He could see her through the big bay window at the front of the house. Once he knew she was okay, he headed home. He hoped to get some sleep that night, with no nightmares.

When he hit the couch at home, his eyes were heavy. He fell asleep before he'd had a chance to change. The dream started. He was in Bella's Victorian home. She kept calling his name. He ran from room to room. No matter where he went, her voice came from another direction. The last place he ran to was the master bedroom, where he found her on the floor with stab wounds in her abdomen. She called out his name one more time before she lost consciousness.

Ian sprang awake, his black T-shirt drenched in sweat. He needed to clean the nightmare off of himself. He headed for the bathroom and spent a long time in the shower. When he exited and grabbed a towel, he could hear his phone ringing in the living room. It was late. No one would call unless it was an emergency. Ian hurried to the phone to see Bella's name flashing across the screen.

"Bella."

"I need your help. Someone is inside my house."

CHAPTER 5

Bella rolled off the blow-up mattress in the master bedroom of her flip. Her back ached from working in the house and sleeping on a mattress on the floor, but she wouldn't let anyone else vandalize her house. Her iPhone screen had a message wishing her sweet dreams, which brought a smile to her face.

Whenever Ian's name crossed her phone, her heart would flutter. That man gave her butterflies with each text message. The next night was their date, and she still needed to find an outfit. He hadn't told her where he planned to take her.

She'd started demolishing the kitchen the previous day, so her coffeepot was next to her blow-up mattress along with a minifridge. Bella had never planned to live in one of her flips, but if she wanted to stay on budget and keep to her timeline, she didn't have time for any more surprise expenses.

The sound of hammers downstairs made her get her butt in gear. That day she and her crew would be finishing the demo in the kitchen. She would move on to the bathroom while her hired hands, Tom and Ed, worked on the second bathroom. One piece of advice she learned from her mentor was to hire a contractor that charged per job and not by the hour. It worked wonderfully. The men she'd hired had shown up each day on time and worked their asses off. If they finished early, they would make more money.

When she rounded the corner into the kitchen, she was surprised by how far the hired hands had gotten. She must have slept through part of the demo.

"Hey, guys."

Ed turned and gave her a nod. He was in his late forties, and like Tom, he'd worked for Bella's old mentor. When Mr. Ainsworth had gone down for what he'd done, his construction crews had lost their jobs. Ed and Tom had struggled to find work. Both had done amazing work in the past, so they were the first people she'd reached out to when she had a flip.

Tom was in his early thirties. When he removed

his shirt, he showed perfectly sculpted abs. The man was sexy as hell, but he didn't make her heart flutter the way Ian did. He almost seemed like a brother to her. In past jobs, he'd gone into detail in explaining how to do certain jobs such as replacing a toilet.

Tom turned his gorgeous smile on her. "Good morning, Bella," he said in his deep Texas drawl. He reached up and wiped the sweat off his brow. Ed continued to take down the old brown wall cabinet.

"Do you think we can finish the kitchen today?" Bella asked. The demo had been fun the first day, but Bella was over it. Her body hurt in parts she hadn't known existed.

Tom surveyed the kitchen. "I think Ed and I can finish the kitchen today. You might want to run to the store and put up some cameras. We had to clean up the front of the house this morning. Someone threw eggs at it. I took pictures and texted them to Officer Anders."

Bella had put motion floodlights on the front porch to help keep the vandals away at night. Cameras were another expense she didn't have money for. Officer Anders wanted her to get them, and Ian asked every night if she'd had them installed.

"Who from Mr. Ainsworth's past do you guys

think would do this? I wasn't the only one that worked for him."

Ed didn't speak very often, so when he answered instead of Tom, Bella was surprised. "Bella, I don't think it's someone from Mr. Ainsworth's past. The people he screwed over had millions. They wouldn't hire someone to throw eggs at your house—they'd hire someone to kill you. Maybe it was someone you outbid on the house. What's that guy's name who overpays and takes all the houses? It could be him."

Ian wouldn't throw eggs at her house. They texted each other each night. Hell, he'd helped her clean up the last mess. Why would he paint the house then stay back and help her? But Ed was right: many of the people Mr. Ainsworth had screwed over were rich. Did she have to worry about having a hit on her head? She could dip into her emergency fund to purchase some cameras. If it saved her from further setbacks, it would be worth it.

"It's not Ian," Bella said. When Tom started to respond, she stopped him. "Ian chased off one of the vandals and made me call the cops. Afterward, he helped me clean up paint off the side of the house. We text every night."

"Like I said, you need cameras. Ed and I got this.

You go get cameras, and we'll help you put them up when you get back."

A half hour later, she stood in front of a display of cameras. The cheapest camera set was a thousand dollars. There was no way could she justify spending a thousand dollars on cameras.

When she turned to leave, a salesman stopped her. He was short—maybe an inch taller than her five-foot-two height. His black-framed glasses were too large for his skinny face. "Can I help you, ma'am?"

"I was looking for some cameras, but these are out of my price range."

He told her to hold on while he ran to the back of the store. She knew the camera gods had worked in her favor today when the skinny geek came out with a box and produced a set of cameras for five hundred dollars.

When Bella left the shop, she noticed a Victoria's Secret store next door. She put the cameras in the back of her trunk and spent the next hour shopping. She found a cute red-lace bra and matching panties. Bella didn't plan to sleep with Ian after their date, but she wanted to feel sexy, and a new bra and panties would do that.

When she got back to her car, her phone vibrated in her pocket. Ava's name flashed across the screen.

"Hey, girl," Bella said.

"How's the flip going? Are you ready for your date tomorrow?"

"Good, and I'm scared out of my mind. I still can't believe he asked me out."

In the background, Bella could hear Ava's heels clicking across the floor. "Don't forget to call me afterward. I want to hear all the delicious details."

Bella switched the call to speakerphone and started her drive home. "I'll call you as soon as the date is over. I'm headed back to the house right now. Ed and Tom are working on the kitchen demo. They plan to help me hang cameras before they head out for the day."

Ava's breath hitched on the other end. "Did something else happen?"

"Someone egged the house. These don't seem like professionals, so I don't think it has to do with Mr. Ainsworth."

"Did you call the cops?"

"Ed sent a picture to Officer Anders, it was only eggs. I'll hang cameras and turn the footage over to the cops if I have another incident."

Ava and Bella talked the rest of the ride back to the house. Bella had shopped longer than she'd planned. The sun was starting to set behind the house. After pulling into the driveway, she sat and stared at the house. She still had to pinch herself each time she looked at it. She couldn't believe she was doing her first big flip. This was the beginning of her new life.

Tom and Ed were sweeping the floor in the kitchen. They'd completed the demo. The flip was ahead of schedule. The earlier Bella finished, the sooner she could get the house listed and make more money, but she wouldn't cut corners for a few extra pennies in her bank account.

"Did you get the cameras?" Tom asked.

Bella held up the box with the cameras inside. Tom nodded and set down his broom. The three of them worked to install the cameras. They took around two hours, and it was dark by the time Tom and Ed left. After a few tweaks, she could see five camera locations on her phone. They'd put all the cameras around the outside of the house. The perp hadn't come inside yet.

She cleaned the debris that remained in the kitchen before she called for pizza. Bella's stomach grumbled as she made the call. She stared down the hallway at the downstairs bathroom, which was next on the list to demolish. If she started that night, she would put herself further ahead of schedule, but she talked herself out of that idea and took a shower before the pizza boy showed up.

When the doorbell rang, Bella used her new app to see who was at the door. She liked the added security she felt with the cameras. The purchase had been a good choice. It didn't take long to grab her pizza and head upstairs to her blow-up mattress. The latest episode of *First Time Flippers* was on. She loved to watch other people work on their houses. The best was when they didn't use a power tool correctly, and the bubble popped up and told the home viewer that what they'd done was wrong.

It wasn't long before Bella fell asleep. She was in the middle of a good dream. Ian had just removed his shirt, and the sun reflected off his toned chest. Bella was about to run her hands up and down his chest when a loud crash woke her from her dream.

The noise brought Bella to her feet. She reached for her app to pull up the video. The feed was black. Whoever had broken the glass downstairs had destroyed her new cameras.

Bella's fingers shook as she called the one person she knew would help her.

"Bella." Ian's rich voice came across the line.

"I need your help. Someone is inside my house."

She could hear fabric rustle in the background. Bella hadn't stopped to see what time it was before calling Ian.

"Did you call the cops?" he asked.

Bella worked her way around the corner and peered down the stairs. "No. I checked the cameras first, and someone blacked them out. You were the first person I thought to call."

A sledgehammer lay on the floor across from the master bedroom. She worked her way over to hammer. She felt better with a weapon in her hands.

"Bella, I'm almost to the house. Go into the closet, and don't come out until you hear my voice. I'm going to call Officer Anders and have him meet me there. Do not leave that room."

"Hurry," she whispered.

She could hear faint footsteps downstairs. She knew she should listen to what Ian said, but the person was still inside the house. With the sledgehammer in her hand, she slid her phone into her pocket and worked her way down the stairs.

The last step creaked under her feet. She held her breath and listened for footsteps. When she didn't hear anything, she slowly worked her way down the hallway till she reached the living room. There, a man was kneeling at the fireplace, jabbing a rod up the chimney.

Bella gripped the sledgehammer with both hands and slowly approached the intruder. She was almost there when the board under her foot squeaked. The man turned. She couldn't see his face because he wore a black ski mask.

He didn't run toward the door—he ran at her. She swung the hammer a second too soon and missed her target. He didn't miss her. The intruder hit her with so much force her head bounced off the floor when she fell backward.

The man jumped on top of her and wrapped his hands around her neck. "Where is the money?" His voice was strained.

Bella couldn't reply while he had his hands around her throat. She kicked her legs, trying to get the intruder off her, but he was double her size, and his arms bulged with muscles. Bella used her nails to claw and try to peel back his hands, but blackness started to take over. In the distance she thought she heard a car door and hoped it was Ian. It would piss him off if she died.

Everything went black.

CHAPTER 6

Ian ignored every speed limit as he weaved his truck through traffic. He kept picturing Bella's lifeless body on the floor, stabbed to death, as it had been in his dreams. He reached for the call button on the steering wheel. He wanted to hear Bella's voice to know she was okay. She hadn't picked up since he'd last spoken with her. Fear coursed through Ian's body. He'd received no intel from Tex yet. Not knowing who was after Bella was his biggest worry.

Ian slammed on the brakes when the light turned red. He impatiently tapped his finger on the armrest. Seconds after the light turned green, he sped through the intersection.

After notifying the cops, he'd called Cole and asked him to meet him at the house. Ian didn't know how he would handle it if Bella was hurt. They'd texted each night asking questions about the other. With each text, he felt closer to her. The previous night, she'd opened up about not having any family. Her mom had passed when she was eighteen, and Mr. Ainsworth took her under his wing. Mr. Ainsworth's kids never came around. Over the years, she'd only spoken to his kids over the phone and never met them in person. Mr. Ainsworth didn't even have a picture of his kids in his office. He had told Bella he considered her more of a daughter than his actual daughter, who only called when she needed something.

When Ian pulled around the corner to Bella's house, it was dark. The police hadn't arrived. He parked in the driveway and pulled his Glock from his holster. In the distance, he could hear sirens. Ian didn't plan to wait for the cops. When he jiggled the knob of the front door, it didn't budge. Using his shoulder, he laid into the door, and it split under the force of his weight.

Ian scanned the room and looked for Bella. A motion to his right caught his eye. A man in a black hoody ran for the back door. When Ian looked down for a second, he saw Bella lying on the floor.

He raised his gun to the man and squeezed the

trigger twice, one shot to each leg. The man's body hit the floor with a thud. Ian ignored the intruder's cries and rushed to Bella's side. He put his fingers to her pulse and let out a sigh of relief when he felt her heartbeat.

He lifted Bella into his arms and cradled her. With his left hand, he lifted her shirt to reassure himself she had no stab wounds. When he heard footsteps on the patio, he prayed it was the medic. Officer Anders burst through the front door.

"He's on the floor in the kitchen," Ian said. He didn't want to leave his spot on the floor with Bella cradled in his arms until he saw her crystal-blue eyes looking at him.

Max nodded, and a trail of officers made their way into the kitchen.

"Sir, I need you to put her down so we can work on her." Two paramedics loomed over him.

Ian gently laid Bella on the floor. Her eyes were still shut. He sat in the folding chair and watched the two paramedics work on her. The woman paramedic said her name was Savanah. He heard the footsteps behind him but didn't take his eyes off Bella. When a hand squeezed his shoulder, he knew his best friend had arrived. Cole didn't need to say anything. Knowing he was by his side was enough for Ian.

Savanah said Bella's vitals were okay. The paramedics had felt a bump on the back of her head, and they talked about the possibility of a concussion. The second paramedic reached into his bag, pulled out a white two-inch packet, and crunched it between his fingers. Ian had seen packets like that before. Smelling salts—he'd carried them in the field. The Navy used them when someone was injured and passed out from the pain. The smelling salts would help wake the injured soldier. The soldiers also used them in pranks because the smell was so bad it could make a person vomit.

Ian held his breath as the paramedics put the packet underneath Bella's nose. It took a few seconds before she groaned softly and opened her eyes. She used her hands to bat the salt from her nose. When she went to rise, the paramedics told her to stay still.

"Bella, my name is Savanah. I'm an EMT with the fire department. Do you know where you are?"

Bella kept closing her eyes. "Yes, my house."

Savanah grabbed a small flashlight from her medical bag. "Bella, I'm going to shine a light in your eyes, and I need you to follow it, okay?" Savanah held each eye open and shined the light in it.

Ian needed Bella to be okay.

After shining the light in Bella's eyes, the paramedics helped her to the folding chair.

"Your throat will hurt for the next twenty-four hours," Savanah said. "If you continue to have issues swallowing or neck pain, go to the emergency room. You also suffered a severe contusion on the back of your head along with a mild concussion. Do you have someone to stay with you? You'll need to be woken up every so often through the night."

Ian didn't give Bella time to reply. "I'll watch over her tonight. Do you think I should take her to the emergency room?"

The contusion was huge. Rage coursed through Ian's body. The intruder deserved more than two bullets to the legs. Ian wanted to slowly dismember his body for what he'd done to Bella. But the paramedics had already carted him out of the house.

"No hospital," Bella whispered.

"You're going."

The paramedics gathered their supplies. "If her symptoms get worse, take her to the hospital."

* * *

Bella rested her hand on Ian's forearm. "Ian, I'm fine. I'll call Ava, and she can come stay with me. Thank you for saving me. If you hadn't made it here in time, I might've died."

Her head buzzed, and her throat felt as though she'd eaten a piece of sandpaper. She had so many questions, and if she went to the hospital, she would have to wait to learn the answers. Most importantly, Bella wanted to know who the intruder was.

"You'll go to my house for the night so I can check on you every few hours." When she started to protest, he held up his hand. "Cole will stay here tonight and board up the back door."

She hadn't even realized Cole had come. When she looked around the room, she saw him standing next to Officer Anders. Bella stood up, preparing to ask the officer for information about who'd broken into her house, but she'd stood too fast. Dizziness took over, and she stumbled.

Ian was by her side in a second, holding her up. "You need to sit down."

"I want to know who that was and why he broke into my house."

Before she knew what happened, Ian swung her up into his arms. She squeaked, "I'm too heavy. Put me down, Ian."

He ignored her demand and carried her across the living room toward the kitchen. Officer Anders and Cole stopped their conversation and stared at the two of them. She couldn't help the blush that crossed her face. Cole raised his eyebrow at his friend.

"Ian, you can put me down," Bella said.

"No."

Cole and Officer Anders let out a chuckle.

"Do you know who it was or why he broke in?" Bella asked.

Officer Anders pinched his brow. "He was screaming in pain and wouldn't answer any of my questions. The hospital will call as soon as he is out of surgery. I'm glad you didn't kill him, Ian. Now we can get answers to why he's been terrorizing her."

Bella could have sworn she heard Ian grumble that he wished the fucker was dead and that next time, he'd take a head shot.

"Ian, can you put me down? I need to start cleaning up the mess. Luckily, it only looks like the back door and this blood on the floor."

"You take care of yourself," Cole said. "I'll take care of the door and the blood. You need rest, and I highly doubt Ian will let you out of his arms for the next few days. I'll also stay here tonight and watch the house. After you meet with the police in the morning, bring me breakfast, and we'll be even."

Adrenaline coursed through Bella's body. She wanted to do something. "I can give my report now."

Ian didn't wait for Officer Anders to respond. He turned and headed for his door and yelled over his shoulder that they would go down to the station in the morning.

If Ian thought he could take charge, he had another thing coming. Bella slapped him on the shoulder. "That was rude to walk away from your friends. I want to get the report over now. You don't need to take care of me. I'll be fine. I can set the alarm to wake me up every hour. And I feel like I could get a bunch of work done."

Ian grunted and headed toward his big truck. He opened the door, placed Bella inside, buckled her in, and kissed her on the forehead. Then he shut the door and climbed in on his side. He gripped the steering wheel and stared out the windshield.

"I thought you were dead, Bella." Ian let out a long sigh. "Can you please come home with me tonight and let me take care of you? If you don't trust me, I can take you to Ava's house. But please let someone look after you. You don't always need to take care of yourself. Lean on me, please."

It wasn't that she didn't trust Ian. She had been on her own for so many years, and after what had happened to her boss, she was scared to lean on someone. But Ian, she knew, wouldn't do anything to hurt her. She'd learned a lot about him in their nightly chats—such as how he didn't like peanut butter. That had almost been a deal breaker until he said he liked it in chocolate.

"I'll go home with you, Ian, but I want to go to the police station first thing in the morning and then head back to the house. I have deadlines I need to make."

Ian nodded and started the truck. They weren't even a mile into the drive when the heaviness of her eyes took over, and she fell asleep. She woke when Ian wrapped his arms around her to pull her out of the truck.

He cradled her in his arms as he walked toward the house. It was a cute ranch-style home. The streetlamps gave enough light for her to see the flowers planted in the front yard and a rocking chair on the front porch. She shouldn't have been surprised by its curb appeal. Bella had stalked the houses Ian had flipped, and the yards were always nice.

Ian opened the front door and walked down a

long hall. She only saw the open kitchen for a second. It looked like a chef's dream with a large island.

Bella was surprised when he set her down on his king-sized bed. "I can sleep in the guest bedroom or the couch," she said.

"No."

There was no point in arguing with the stubborn man. Bella worked her shoes off. When he came back toward the bed, he had a T-shirt and boxers for her to wear.

It looked as if Ian wanted to help her change, but she put her foot down. "I can dress myself."

Ian paused, probably trying to decide whether he should fight her on this or not. He finally nodded and headed toward the door. Bella went into the bathroom. She spotted toothpaste on the counter and used her finger to clean her teeth. She didn't want to have bad breath when her knight showed back up.

When she got back to the room, Ian was standing next to the bed with a glass of water in his hand.

"Here's some water and a Tylenol."

She took the glass from him. The cold water felt good on her sore throat. She crawled into his bed.

Ian leaned down and kissed her on the forehead. "Good night, Bella. I'll wake you in a couple hours."

But she didn't want him to go. "Please stay."

Ian stripped down to his boxers. It was hard to see his body in the darkness. When he climbed into bed and pulled her body against his, she felt his hard chest against her back. She stilled in his arms when she felt his erection.

"Go to sleep, Bella." His voice held a hint of laughter.

She fell asleep and dreamed of the sexy man in bed with her.

CHAPTER 7

Ian poured another cup of coffee. Bella was sound asleep in his bed. Like a crazy person, he'd watched her sleep most of the night. He was worried that he wouldn't wake up to check her, so he'd stayed up all night with his arms around her and a painful boner.

His phone chimed on the counter. Officer Anders had messaged him to let him know he was at the station. Ian enjoyed another sip of caffeine then padded down the hall toward his room. Bella's blond hair covered his pillow. He didn't want to wake her—she looked so peaceful.

Slowly, he ran his hand down the side of her face and watched her crystal-blue eyes open. "Good morning, Bella. How do you feel?"

She stretched her arms above her head, causing

the T-shirt to ride up. The creamy-white skin of her stomach showed. Ian wanted to run his tongue over her body.

"I feel like a Mack truck ran me over. You don't happen to have coffee, do you?"

Ian leaned down and lightly brushed her lips. He hadn't planned to do it. Bella stiffened under his lips for a second, but when he went to pull back, she wrapped her arms around his neck and pulled him in tighter. When he swiped his tongue across her lips, she gave him entrance. He ran his hand up and down the side of her body. If he didn't pull back soon, he would take her right there, and he wanted to wine and dine her first. Bella also had suffered an injury the day before.

When Ian pulled back, she whined. "You need to get ready," he said. "Officer Anders is waiting for us." He leaned down one more time and kissed the top of her nose.

He watched as she headed toward the bathroom and groaned when she put an extra sway in her hips. She let out a giggle, knowing what she did to him.

A cold shower called his name. He used the guest bathroom. Being around Bella for the past twelve hours had his dick permanently hard. Ian leaned against the shower wall as the cold water rained down on him. It did nothing to relieve the pressure. He wrapped his hands around his cock, seeing images of Bella spread out across his bed. Her plump breasts called to him. He gripped himself harder as he imagined her hands running over his body. Ian exploded within a minute. He hadn't come that fast since he was a teenager.

After quickly drying off, he headed to the kitchen to make Bella breakfast. He had one pancake left to flip when she walked into the kitchen with only a towel wrapped around her body and another towel around her hair. It didn't matter that he'd jacked off ten minutes earlier—his dick sprang back to life.

He'd put her clothes in the washer the night before. She had nothing to wear. Ian rushed to the laundry room to retrieve her clothes. If she didn't get dressed soon, she would end up on the counter.

When he came back into the kitchen, Bella had taken the last pancake off the grill. She looked so perfect in his kitchen. He would make it his mission to have her in his house permanently one day.

"I washed these for you last night."

She reached for the clothes in his hands. "Thank you." She turned to walk down the hallway and dropped the towel. Her perfect ass was on display.

Ian let out a groan. He knew what he would jack off to that night.

* * *

"There's a dead body in my chimney?" Bella screeched at Officer Anders. How the hell would she sell a house with a dead body? *Fuck.* Who would remove the dead body?

"There *was* a dead body. A team removed it from the chimney, along with a million dollars."

Bella was happy that she'd decided not to remodel the chimney herself. She'd thought about asking Ian for help because he seemed interested in it. She would have had a heart attack if the body had come out when he was working on it.

Ian squeezed her hand. "Do you know who the dead person is?"

"Yes, it was the previous owner's daughter. The man who broke into the house was the previous owner's son. His sister caught him trying to put the money in the chimney, and when she said she would tell their parents about it, he got pissed and hit her too hard. He said he hadn't meant to kill her. After that, he stuck her body in the chimney along with the money."

Chills came over her. "Why did he wait until now?"

"The day after he killed his sister, SAPD picked him up for having a hundred grams of cocaine with the intent to sell. He got sentenced to ten years in jail, but with the overcrowding, he got out early and wanted his money. You won't have to worry about him anymore. With the attempted murder and breaking his parole, he's looking at thirty years in jail."

Bella told Officer Anders her account of what had happened. The officer said she might need to show up to his trial, but he had a feeling they would cut a deal if the guy told them who the money belonged to and who'd helped him steal it. The judge could cut his sentence to twenty-five years. Either way, the guy was out of Bella's life for good.

After speaking with Officer Anders, Bella and Ian stopped by the diner to pick up food for Cole. Bella didn't want her time with Ian to end. They'd originally set a date for that night, but she didn't know whether he still planned on taking her out or if he'd decided she was too much to deal with.

Ian was quiet after leaving the diner, and Bella didn't know what he was thinking. He finally broke the tension in the cab. "What has you so lost in thought?"

"Are we still going out tonight? I know what happened last night was a lot, but I still wanted to go out with you. I totally understand if you don't. My life seems to be a little crazy at the moment—"

Ian put a hand on her thigh and squeezed. "That was a lot of information at once. Yes, we are still going out tonight. Your life seems exciting, and it didn't scare me away. I did almost have a heart attack when I saw your lifeless body. But none of it has scared me away."

"Okay." Bella wanted to jump up and down, but she played it cool instead.

When they arrived at her house, Cole's truck sat in the driveway. They walked into the living room and saw Cole halfway up the chimney.

"Hey, Cole, it's Bella and me. We brought you food."

He came out from the chimney, covered in dirt and grime. His blond hair was black, and his white shirt was full of soot.

Bella rushed to the garage and brought back a wet cloth for him to run over his face.

"Thank you, Bella. The fireplace should work now. After the detectives left with the body, I worked to remove the remaining debris and cleaned the chimney. It's back in working order."

"Thank you." She ran up and gave him a hug and heard Ian growl behind her. Cole wrapped his arms around her and pulled her in tighter.

Ian came up and pulled her from Cole's embrace. "Fucker. Find your own woman."

Cole winked at her. "I like yours."

Over the next hour, as they ate lunch, the banter continued between Cole and Ian. Bella hadn't laughed so hard in years. When they were done eating, Cole excused himself and headed home. After he left, the sexual tension between Ian and Bella filled the house. Ian helped her clean up the remaining mess from the chimney, and they kept accidentally touching.

When they finished, Ian wrapped her in his arms. "Why don't you go get ready? I'll be back in an hour, and we can have our date."

"Where are we going?"

"It's a surprise. Wear a skirt."

* * *

Bella couldn't hold her excitement as Ian turned into the parking lot at Travis Park. The far end of the park had a huge movie screen. She would get to experience an outdoor movie. She'd always wanted to do something like that.

Ian turned off the car and told her to stay put. He hurried to the other side, helped her down from the truck, and grabbed a picnic basket from the back. They picked a spot close to the back, and he laid out a blanket on the grass.

She didn't care what movie was on. As long as Ian put his arms around her, she was happy. Her date pulled out her favorite movie snacks—Reese's Peanut Butter Cups and popcorn. The best way to her heart was with chocolate and salt.

The movie started at dusk. Bella wrapped herself around Ian. She felt so comfortable in his arms. Halfway through the movie, he pulled her head back and pressed his lips to hers. He tossed the corner of the blanket over her lower body.

Ian worked his hand up her leg and traced the outside of her thong. He deepened the kiss to capture the moans coming from her mouth. He slipped his hands under her thong. When he pressed his fingers to her clit, she was close to coming. Ian dipped his fingers lower, and when he went inside her, she couldn't hold back the moan. He worked his fingers inside her and brushed her clit, and she had the most powerful orgasm.

Bella blushed hotly. She couldn't believe she'd come in public. When she looked around, no one appeared to be watching them.

"Don't worry, Bella. Nobody saw you come on my hand."

She cuddled in closer for the rest of the movie.

Later, when he escorted her to her door, she thought he would come in. Instead, he leaned in and kissed her on the lips. "Good night, Bella."

"You don't want to come in?"

"Oh, I want to come in, but if I do, you'll end up naked. I want a few more dates before that."

He leaned in one more time and kissed her before heading toward his truck.

When Bella closed the door, she heard her phone chime. It was a message from Ian: *When you touch yourself tonight, think about me. I will be thinking about you and how you came apart in my hands.*

CHAPTER 8

"What time are you coming over tonight?" Ian asked.

For the past two weeks, they'd tried to see each other each day. When they couldn't find time to meet, they would talk on the phone. The night before, they'd talked until two in the morning. The conversation had flowed, and she hadn't realized how late it was until she heard Ian yawn.

Bella looked around the flip. She was almost done. She would make her deadline of Friday and schedule an open house for Sunday. "I think I'll be done around five. Is that too early?"

"No. Cole is about to finish the cabinet install. After lunch, we were going to drive by a couple of houses."

Bella knew one of the houses he planned to look at. She'd seen it hit the county courthouse website that morning. She wanted to drive by and see if it could be her next flip. If everything went according to her plan, she would sell her current house next week. Ava had said a couple of people were already interested.

"Are you driving by the house on Lake Circle?"

Ian hummed on the other end. "Do you want to look at it with me? We could maybe do the next flip together."

In theory, it sounded like a good idea, but Bella wanted to make it on her own. She'd worked with someone before, and it hadn't turned out well. Oh, she knew Ian wouldn't betray her as Mr. Ainsworth had, but she also loved to talk about her day with him. She didn't know how it would be to work with someone and date him too. Especially when flipping houses was stressful.

"Nope. May the best woman win the bid."

Ian's rich laughter boomed through the phone. "If you say so."

"I will distract you with my body during the bidding." A whole outfit popped into her mind. She would wear a pair of booty shorts and a white tight tank top with no bra. It would distract Ian from the auction, and she'd get the bid. Too bad she hadn't thought of that idea twenty houses before.

"Whenever you are near me, I'm distracted. You are the most beautiful woman."

Bella swooned at his words. "You're not too bad yourself. What did you have planned for tonight?"

A loud crash echoed through the phone. "Sorry, let me step outside. Have you ever watched the bats fly out from under the bridge in Austin?"

"Nope." She'd heard about the bats. When the sun set, two million of them flew out from under the bridge. The only thing Bella could think about was that the first thing she did when she woke up was go potty. Wouldn't the bats do the same thing? "Will they poop on me? Because driving an hour and a half to get pooped on doesn't sound like fun."

Ian let out a chuckle. "We'll stand so they won't fly over us. You will be poop free."

"Sure, but if they poop on me, I'll be mad. Will we make it in time if we don't leave until five?"

"Yes, sunset is around eight. I promise to protect you from the guano. And Bella, don't forget to pack a bag."

A wave of excitement coursed through her. "Are we staying in Austin, or am I sleeping at your house?" It didn't really matter where they stayed.

Over the past two weeks, the sexual tension had increased. Ian had wanted to wait to make sure she was ready. The man didn't understand that she'd wanted him the first day she laid eyes on him.

"I rented us a hotel room in downtown, so we could walk to the bridge and then go to a jazz bar and listen to music."

"A girl could get used to this."

"I can't wait to get my hands on you tonight."

"Me too," she said. "You've been driving me crazy."

"Just wait until I've got you spread out on the bed, panting my name. I will spend hours feasting on that pussy. Just thinking about you has me hard. I don't think I've ever taken so many cold showers since I met you."

Ian's deep voice, with the added talk about sex, turned her on. She wanted to climb through the phone. "That's a lot of talk and no action yet."

Ian huffed. "I'll be at your house at five. Bye, Bella."

Bella had a hard time concentrating on hanging the new bathroom towel fixture. Her mind kept wandering back to Ian and his muscles and his lips.

* * *

Ian and Bella were back in the hotel. The latest episode of *The Profit* was on TV. Ian yelled at the business owners for all the financial mistakes they'd made. Bella should have been tired from the long day, but excitement about what might come next coursed through her.

They'd arrived in Austin a little before eight o'clock. Bella and Ian worked their way through the crowd and got a spot right on the edge. At almost exactly eight o'clock, Bella heard a few squeaks coming from below. Before she had time to ask Ian what was about to happen, a black stream flowed from underneath the bridge. She'd read on her way up to Austin that approximately two million bats would fly out. It was one thing to read it, but seeing it was amazing and a little creepy. Bella didn't know whether it was from her years of watching scary shows or the books she'd read, but for a second, she thought the cloud of bats would turn into a vampire.

The stream of bats took about forty-five minutes. Bella watched the people below. She couldn't believe people paid to sit in canoes so the bats could fly over them. For her, the thought of getting crapped on or bitten by a bat would have stopped any idea of sitting in a canoe underneath the bridge.

After watching the stream of bats, Ian and Bella

walked to a local jazz restaurant. They ordered wine and dinner. When the waiter asked if she wanted dessert, she said no.

Bella had butterflies in her stomach. She was ready to get back to the room. When she and Ian had made it back to the hotel, Bella had grabbed his hand and led him to the bedroom.

* * *

Ian couldn't wait to see Bella's naked body. It wasn't the first time he'd seen glimpses of her. He really liked Bella. A lot. And that night, they would take their relationship to the next level. He'd followed her into the bedroom and couldn't wait to run his hands over her body.

He stalked to where Bella stood next to the bed in her flowing white dress. He reached his hands around her neck and unclasped her dress. It fell from her shoulders, exposing her beautiful body. Bella held her lip between her teeth. He reached up with his thumb to pull her lip free, and she nipped him, sending a jolt straight to his groin.

Her delicate hands grabbed the bottom of his T-shirt and slowly worked it up to his chest as she dragged her fingers along his skin and took the shirt off his body. Her touch alone almost made him lose control.

He stepped back to gaze at the woman in front of him. She was breathtaking. He ran his finger along the red lace strap of her bra and worked it over the edge of her shoulder. Goose bumps formed on her skin. He unhooked the bra behind her back, and when her bra fell to the floor, he leaned in and took one of her nipples in his mouth. He heard a wisp of a whimper, and when he sucked harder, she rested her dainty hands on his shoulder to keep herself up.

Ian stepped back to look at Bella. She was even more breathtaking than he could imagine. "You're so beautiful, Bella."

She ran her hands over his chest. "Why am I the only naked one?"

Before he had time to respond, Bella's hands went to his belt, and she slowly worked his pants down. Instead of standing back up, she pulled his boxers down and wrapped her hands around his length. Her hands were like velvet.

He closed his eyes for a second to control his body, but when Bella wrapped her warm lips around him, he almost lost it. He twined his hands through her hair and pulled her head back for a second. Ian didn't want to embarrass himself in the first few seconds.

Bella leaned back on her heels and turned her crystal-blue eyes on him. "Did I do something wrong?"

"No, it felt so good." She leaned forward again and captured his length back in her mouth. Her warm, velvety tongue had his body on fire. Ian kept a hand wound in her hair to control her pace. When she cupped his balls, he rested his free hand on the bed. Bella raised her crystal-blue eyes and took his length deeper.

That image would be engraved forever in his mind. Bella on her knees in front of him was more beautiful than he could ever have imagined. He couldn't take his eyes off her while she worked his length in and out of her mouth.

When she took him deep into her throat, he couldn't take it any longer. He pulled her from her knees and tossed her on the bed. Her hands went to her breasts to cover herself.

"Don't, Bella. You are beautiful, and I want to see every last inch of you."

A light blush appeared on Bella's chest. "I feel exposed."

"Bella, it's only me..." Ian crawled up her body

and placed a kiss on her hip bone. "And you." He worked his hand up the side of her body and cupped her breast with his left hand. Ian slowly ran his finger over her hard nipple. When her body arched into his touch, he worked his way closer until he'd wrapped his lips around her nipple.

Bella ran her hands through Ian's hair, tugging him closer. She moaned when his lips went around her right nipple. He dragged the breast-free hand down her body and slipped his fingers into her wet channel. Bella was ready for him. Her clit was hard, and when he brushed it with his thumb, her body arched off the bed and tried to get more contact.

"More," she whispered.

"More what?"

Bella let out a frustrated breath. "Please, Ian. I need you."

Ian was close to losing control, but he wanted to taste her. He grabbed Bella's ankles and threw them over his shoulders. When he reached her velvety fold, Ian licked her. Bella's hips came off the bed, but he grabbed her slim hip bones and held her in place. When she stopped moving, he used his hands to stroke her folds.

The moan that left her lips came out as a whimper. She reached down and pulled him up. "I need you, Ian. My body is on fire."

Ian nibbled on her ear as he pushed forward and was rewarded with her tight channel. It felt so good that his vision almost went black. Once he was fully in her, he stopped.

"Move, Ian."

Ian slowly worked his length in and out of her. One arm, stretched above Bella's head, braced him, and he used his other hand to cup her breast. As soon as he ran his thumb over her nipple, her eyes rolled back in her head.

"Ian, I'm close," she whispered.

He reached down between them and pinched her clit. Her body exploded the second he touched her, and her channel clenched Ian so tightly he couldn't hold back any longer. He continued to move until both of their orgasms had stopped.

They lay in silence. The only sound was their heavy breathing. After a minute, Ian rolled to the side and pulled Bella back to his chest. What they'd done was magical, and he would never let her go.

Ian pulled her hair to the side and kissed her neck.

"I like you, Ian," she said, but he knew what she really meant.

"I like you too, Bella. Now, get some sleep because I will wake you up in an hour."

And he did. Ian woke Bella up many times throughout the night, and each time was better than the last.

CHAPTER 9

Bella couldn't help but smile as she sat out on the balcony of their room and watched the traffic go by. Austin was one of her favorite cities. Everyone around her was friendly and inviting. Ian was in the shower. She insisted on him taking a shower alone. He'd woken her up three times during the night. If she went into the shower with him, they would never leave the hotel.

Ian's phone chimed beside her.

"Hey, Bella, can you read me the text? I'm waiting on something from Cole."

When she turned to look inside the hotel room, she caught sight of Ian drying his body off. The man was sexy as hell. She reached for the phone and keyed in his password. She stared at the message for a few seconds and clicked the attachment.

This can't be right. Why would he do this? she thought. She paged through the attachment. It got hard to read because of the tears forming in her eyes.

He walked up behind her and put a hand on her shoulder. But she didn't want him to touch her. After what she'd seen, she never wanted to see the prick again.

Bella faced Ian, handed him his phone, and started packing.

"What did it say?" Ian's brows furrowed in confusion. He glanced down at his phone.

Bella couldn't stop the tears that streamed down her face. It had only been two weeks, but her heart was already in his hands, and he'd ripped it apart. When he looked up, his face was pale.

She didn't give him time to speak. "How could you?" she screamed.

"This is not what it looks like." Ian tried to touch her, and she flinched away. She saw the hurt in his eyes, but what he'd done was uncalled for and maybe unforgivable.

She stopped packing her bag and gave him her full attention. "You're saying you didn't have someone dig into every part of my past?"

He ran a hand through his hair. "Bella, stop for a second and let me explain."

"What is there to explain? I fell for you and trusted you with my heart. And what did you do? You betrayed that trust by having someone dig into my life. I'm an open book—you could have asked me anything. Instead, you hired someone. The only reason I can think of right now is that you think I helped Mr. Ainsworth."

Ian clenched his hands at his sides. "Bella, I didn't do this to find information out on you. I was trying to help you."

Bella reached up and swiped the tears from her eyes. "I need time. If I stay in the same room with you a second longer, I will say something I'll regret."

"We can talk about it on our way back to San Antonio."

There was no way she would get in his truck and sit next to him for an hour. She needed time to think, and she couldn't think when he was near. She might forgive him, but at the moment, she was in no mood to forgive. He'd ruined something special. He'd turned one of the most magical nights of her life into something dirty. She felt not only betrayed but used as well.

"No, I'm taking a taxi back."

"Bella, that's stupid. I can drive you or take my truck. You aren't safe in a taxi."

She let out a bitter laugh. "Oh, but you're safe to be around." She walked up and poked him in the chest. "You invaded my privacy."

Bella turned on her heel and walked toward the door. Ian put his hand against the door.

"Bella, don't go. You need to listen."

"If you want to save any part of what we have, you will remove your hand."

Ian removed his hand from the door as if it burned him. When she took one last look in his eyes, he looked almost as torn as she did.

When she pulled the door open, he asked, "Can we talk tomorrow?"

"I don't know, Ian. Give me time."

She walked out of the hotel room and grabbed the first taxi she could find to take her home. Bella curled up in the back of the taxi and cried the whole way back to San Antonio. She cried because she'd lost the man she had fallen for in a short time. She cried because she wished her mom was alive so she would have someone to talk to. She cried because she felt like she'd made the biggest mistake of her life.

CHAPTER 10

It's not what you think. Ian's words echoed in her mind.

Bella hadn't moved from the blow-up mattress in the master bedroom. After she got home the previous day, she walked past the contractors and up to the room then curled up in a ball and cried. The last time she'd cried that hard was when she lost her mom to cancer. She'd heard the workers downstairs, but she couldn't bring herself to face anyone.

Luckily, today she would be home alone because the contractors didn't work on Sundays. Her head hurt from crying all night, and her eyes felt tender. Bella couldn't understand how Ian could betray her. He'd made her laugh, and she felt protected with him, even though sometimes his overprotectiveness had pissed her off.

Bella turned on her phone. Message after message appeared on the screen. She couldn't get herself to read them yet. She went to the bathroom and took a shower. She could hear another ding coming through. It was time to face the world.

Ian: *Bella, I need to know you made it back.*

Ian: *Bella, please call.*

Ian: *I drove by, and I know you are back safe.*

That made him sound like a stalker.

Ian: *I'm not giving up, Bella.*

Ian: *I had Tex look into your past when you were getting attacked. I tried to figure out who was after you. It wasn't for my reading enjoyment.*

Could she believe him? Had he done it to help find whoever was after her? It made more sense than him looking into her background because he was suspicious about her.

Ava: *Hey, girl, I want all the deets.*

Ian: *Good night, Bella.*

Ava: *You better call me.*

Bella wasn't quite ready to forgive Ian. She picked up the phone and dialed Ava's number.

Her friend answered on the second ring. "I've

been trying to get a hold of you for twenty-four hours. What did he do, lock you in a room?"

"Well, hello to you too."

"I want deets, woman. Did you have fun?"

Bella picked at her leggings and wondered how much she should tell her friend. She needed someone to tell her problems to. "It started out amazing. The bat thing was really cool, and then we went to a jazz bar and spent the rest of the night in bed."

"I hear sadness in your voice. Was he that bad in bed?"

The tears started to leak from Bella's eyes. "No, he was amazing. But the next morning, he received a text."

"From a girlfriend?" Ava shouted.

"No, from some guy with an attachment that held my whole life. He had me investigated, Ava, down to my high school GPA."

When Ava didn't answer right away, Bella looked at the phone to make sure they were still connected.

"Did he tell you why?" Ava finally asked.

"At the time, I didn't give him a chance. He invaded my privacy, and I thought he did it because he thought I knew what Mr. Ainsworth did."

"I've met Ian a couple times. He doesn't seem like the type of person to just invade your privacy."

Bella let out a huff. "You're supposed to be on my side."

"I am, but I also want what's best for you, and Ian made you happy."

"I turned my phone off yesterday for a few hours. I figured I would have caved if he kept calling. I just turned it back on. And… he said he had someone look into my past when people were after me."

Ava hummed on the other end. "Now, that sounds like him. When are you going to go apologize?"

"In a few hours. I want to work around the house first. I need a little more time to think."

"Don't think too long. Go have great makeup sex, and call me tomorrow so we can talk about plans to list the house."

Ava was right. Ian looking into her past to protect her sounded more like him than looking into it because she'd done something wrong. The look of disappointment in his eyes had haunted her the night before when she'd tried to fall asleep, and she'd reached for her phone numerous times but hadn't called him. Now she wished she had.

After hanging up with Ava, Bella walked downstairs to see what work had been completed the day before. She stopped dead when she came to the kitchen. Happy tears formed in her eyes. She'd ordered white cabinets to offset the dark wood counters, but what caught her eye was the new window above the sink, which looked out into the backyard. The added window brought natural light into the room. Bella had wanted to capture the essence of the Victorian home and add touches a chef would die for, so she'd also had a six-burner gas stove installed.

She ran her hands over the countertops and couldn't help squealing with excitement. The house was close to being done. In the bathroom, the contractor had laid the white-marble tile, and the claw-foot tub sat against the far wall. White flooring contrasted perfectly with the light blue walls. Bella couldn't help herself—she climbed into the tub to see how it felt.

Bella had brought contractors in to get the house done more quickly. She'd dipped further than she wanted into her savings, but if she could sell the house fast, it would work out. Ava had sent her comps for the area a few days ago, and Bella planned to make a huge profit on the house.

None of the other houses in the neighborhood

had as much square footage as her Victorian home. She'd renovated both bathrooms and the kitchen. The other rooms had fresh paint and re-sanded hardwood floors. If the schedule stayed intact, she could list the house at the end of next week.

When she passed by the fireplace, an image of Ian helping her clean up the mess brought back a good memory. She had so many good memories of their time together over the past few weeks. Bella already ached to go back. She planned to listen to his side of the story, but she would make him wait it out. He didn't need to know she'd caved within twenty-four hours of being mad.

A loud knock at the front door startled her. When she swung the door open, she expected to see Ian on the other side. Instead, a man and woman stood there. The man wore a dark suit. He was on the skinnier side and not much taller than her five-two frame. The woman towered over both of them. Her tight red dress fit her model figure.

"Hello. Can I help you?" Bella asked. She kept the door partially closed.

The woman was the first to speak. She seemed irritated and tapped her toes against the porch floor. "We would like to look at the house."

Bella knew Ava had planned to send feelers out

to other real estate agents. But she'd expected them to call, not show up and demand a showing, especially since the house still needed more work.

"Please excuse my partner. It been a long day. My name is Ryan Smith, and this is Tina Jones. We've been eyeing this house for a while for one of our clients, and we saw that it's going on the market soon. We hoped if our client liked it to make a high offer and keep it off the market."

Looking over their shoulders, Bella saw a red Maserati next to her car. It would be a dream come true if she'd already found a buyer for the house. The first person she thought she would want to tell was Ian. He would be proud of her. But he still needed to grovel before she completely forgave him.

"Please come in."

Tina breezed by her with her high heels clicking across the hardwood. The woman needed an attitude adjustment, but if Bella sold the house, dealing with the bitch would be worth it.

They gathered in the living room, and Bella explained what she had changed and what she had kept original. She detailed how she'd kept the original Victorian mantel and updated the fireplace with a whitewash. The tour continued throughout the house and ended in the kitchen.

"Jesus Christ, how long are you going to keep up the charade?" Tina asked.

Everyone was quiet for a second before Ryan pulled out a gun and pointed it at Bella.

Fuck, she thought. *This house will be the death of me. Two attempts on my life within a month.* "Do you always point guns at someone when making an offer on a house?"

Tina tapped her fingers on the wood countertops. The sound echoed through the house. "We aren't here to buy the house. We are here for you."

Cold washed over Bella as she stared down the gun pointed at her. She reached for her phone in her back pocket, and it wasn't there. Earlier, after talking to Ava, she'd left it in her bedroom.

"I don't understand what you want from me. The house isn't overpriced." It was hard for Bella to keep her voice from shaking. She started to slowly walk backward toward the stairs. If she could make it to her room, everything would be okay.

"Stop." Ryan's hands shook.

Tina walked up next to him and pulled the gun from his hands. She looked as if she had done this a few times. "Cuff the bitch. We have a plane to catch, and she is wasting my time."

If Bella had learned anything from her two

classes in self-defense, it was *never get caught,* and *run whenever possible.* She should have kept up with the classes. *Damn.* As with all fitness classes, she'd started well the first week and stopped by the second.

"Please put your hands out."

The fucker had actually said "please." Tina rolled her eyes at Ryan, and her movement distracted him for a second. Bella used the opportunity to run toward the living room. She didn't get more than three feet before the gun fired. The bullet missed her by a millimeter. Bella stopped in her tracks. There was no way she would outrun the gun. Ryan tackled her from behind, and she hit the floor with enough force to knock the wind out of her. Before she had time to fight back, he wrapped a zip tie around her hands.

Ryan and Tina shoved her out the front door. If the intruder hadn't pressed a gun to her spine, she would have tried to call out to the neighbors. Ryan popped the trunk when they neared the car.

"I'll be good. Please don't put me in there," Bella said, but her begging landed on deaf ears.

Tina shoved her in with such force that Bella lost her footing and smacked her head on the side of the trunk. Darkness crept into her vision, and her head pounded. When the trunk door closed, she became terrified. Who were these people, and what did they want?

Bella closed her eyes for a couple of seconds and tried to get her nerves under control. Her head pounded from when she'd hit the side of the trunk, but she needed to power through the pain. It was hard to see inside the trunk. Bella remembered that most trunks had a lever to pop them open. She worked from one side to the other and felt the inside of the trunk. The lever wasn't there.

Bella couldn't hold the sob in any longer. She felt defeated. She let the tears run down her face. Was this how she would die—at the hands of two idiots?

No. She would fight. She used her foot to kick where the taillight was. If she could break the back taillight, she might be able to flag down a car. She kicked at it for the next twenty minutes. Ryan and Tina hadn't said where they were going, so she didn't know how much time she had left. Right when she was about to give up, the taillight split. She pounded the rest of the light off the car and peered through the hole she'd created.

Her heart sank. They had pulled into a private airfield. Bella recognized it from times when she had flown with Mr. Ainsworth. She grabbed one of the glass shards from the taillight to use as a weapon for when they opened the trunk. She needed to fight.

How long would it be before someone noticed she was missing? The crew wouldn't show up until Monday. Ian knew she was mad at him. Whoever had her would have more than a twenty-four-hour head start. And would the crew notice she wasn't there Monday, or would they think she was with Ian? If she made it out of this, she planned to never storm away from Ian again, even if he was an asshole.

Car doors slammed, and Bella knew her time to fight was about to come up. She had the glass shard in front of her, ready to swing at the first person. When the trunk door opened, she surged forward and dug the shard into Ryan's stomach.

She didn't have time to pull back and attack Tina. The woman took the butt of the gun and brought it down on Bella's head. Pain radiated across her head, and darkness followed.

CHAPTER 11

Ian couldn't believe he hadn't told Tex he didn't need the file any longer. *Fuck.* The file wasn't for his enjoyment—he wanted to catch the person who was after Bella. Ian no longer needed the file since Jake was behind bars. Why couldn't Bella stop and listen for two seconds?

"Why don't you go talk to her?" Cole asked.

Ian had broken down and called his friend that morning to ask him to come over. The house had seemed so empty, and he'd needed someone to talk to about his major fuckup.

The Eagles versus the Cowboys football game played in the background. Normally, when the Eagles scored, it brought a smile to his face, but he couldn't concentrate on the game. He was too worried about Bella.

"She wants nothing to do with me."

Cole rolled his eyes and took a swig of his beer. "Stop being a drama queen. Pick up some roses and chocolates, and go grovel."

It was the tenth time they'd had that same discussion. Ian glanced at the clock. He hadn't talked to Bella in more than twenty-four hours. It felt like a lifetime. Ian knew it was his fault. He was the only one to blame that the woman he'd fallen for had walked out of his life.

Ian picked up his phone and dialed her again. It went straight to voicemail. She'd powered her phone off to ignore his calls. "What happens if she doesn't open the door?"

"Grow a pair. If she doesn't answer, knock until she does."

Cole was right. He would grovel and pester her until she either told him to fuck off or listened to him. Ian sat through the rest of the game. The need to rush to be at her side intensified, but he wanted to give her time to think and not be so pissed off when he showed up.

Once the game ended, Ian practically ran to his truck. He figured she was at her flip. She spent any spare hours at that house. With her extra time and the contractor she'd brought in, he imagined she would have the house done on Friday. She could pull the flip off within a month. Ian was proud of her and enjoyed helping her when he had the time.

He grabbed a bouquet and a bag of Reese's Peanut Butter Cups. When he pulled into her drive-way, he took a couple of deep breaths. Ian walked past her car in the driveway. He noticed that the door was cracked open as he approached it. After the vandalism, Bella had always locked the door.

The hairs on the back of his neck rose. Ian knocked on the door, and it swung open. When he didn't hear footsteps or noises, he shouted her name through the house. Nothing. He walked to each room and continued shouting her name. There was no answer. No one was at the house.

When he walked back into the master bedroom, he noticed her purse on the floor. He looked inside and found her phone. Something was wrong. He powered the phone back on, guessing her password on the first try. It was the date she'd bought the new house. A slew of messages appeared across her screen, all from him.

Ian scrolled through her contacts until found Ava's number. Ava was Bella's best friend and would know where she might have gone. His finger hesitated over her number for a second. Ian knew in his gut something was off. He pressed the button.

Ava answered on the second ring. “Hey, chicky. Are you already done with makeup sex?”

“Ava, this is Ian.”

“Is Bella okay?”

While Ian had the phone pressed to his ear, he continued to search the house in case he’d missed a clue. He couldn’t turn off the sick feeling in his stomach. “I don’t know. We had a fight yesterday, and when I came to her house to grovel, the front door was open, and her purse and phone were left behind. I have a feeling something happened.”

Ava covered the phone. Ian could hear muffled voices as she spoke to someone. Ava came back on the line. “Ethan and I are on our way over. Don’t do anything stupid.”

Ian clicked off the phone and sat on the chair in the living room. Horrible scenarios ran through his brain. His dream of Bella’s dead body on the floor came to the forefront. Tex had set up a program that would send Ian a text if Jake got out of jail. Ian hadn’t received a text from it yet. He sent a text to Tex just to make sure, and not more than a minute later, Tex replied and let him know Jake was in jail.

A ding on his phone alerted him with another text from Tex: *What's going on?*

Ian answered: *Bella's missing.*

Tex called immediately, and Ian relayed the little information he had about how their fight and how he'd gone to apologize and found her house empty. Tex told him he would work to pull off images from cameras around the area to see if he could find anything. He had new facial-recognition software he could use to pinpoint her face in the San Antonio area.

During the conversation with Tex, Cole texted to see how Ian's grovel had gone. Ian sent a quick text to update him, and Cole responded that he was on his way over.

It felt as if an hour passed before Ian heard the car doors slamming outside. He heard multiple cars, and the swarm of people that came through the door startled him. Ava was the first to enter, followed by her fiancé, Ethan, who worked for the FBI. Officer Max Anders followed behind Ethan. Cole brought up the rear.

Max ran his hand through his hair. "On the way over, I contacted the jail where Jake is locked up. Bella wouldn't run away, and we can't file a missing person's report for another few hours."

"I contacted one of my friends to hack into the street cameras," Ian said. "Once he gets a hit, he plans to call."

Helplessness washed over Ian. Was this how his fellow soldiers felt when his unit went missing? Twenty-six hours had passed since she'd walked out of the hotel. If someone had kidnapped her, they'd need to find her soon. Studies showed that most kidnapped victims were killed within the first twenty-four hours. If Ian hadn't made Bella mad, she would have had her phone on her, and Tex could have tracked her.

"Stop beating yourself up," Ava said. "We will find her."

Before Ian could respond, his phone rang. It was Tex.

"You're on speaker," Ian said.

Tex went straight to the point. "My software picked her up on a private airstrip outside San Antonio. I traced the car backward, and it came from her house. They had shoved her in the trunk."

"Who?"

He could hear the sound of fingers on a keyboard. "They have a tech person working for them. He buried the flight plan. I called Beth in to help, but it will take us both a while to dig through the trail. I'm running their faces now. Nothing has come up yet. Ian, these people have money. I think we need to cross-reference them against Mr. Ainsworth."

Ethan stepped forward. "We have a few hours before the federal prison visiting hours end. Why not try to speak to Mr. Ainsworth?"

Tex said, "That's a good idea. I know the warden of that prison. I'll call and have them make sure you can see him. Also, did you look through the file I sent you?"

That fucking file was why they were in a predicament in the first place. If he hadn't requested it, she would be in his arms. He would be cuddled up the couch with her right now instead of trying to figure out who'd kidnapped her.

"The file's on my phone. I never opened it. Fuck." He ran his hand through his hair. "Bella saw the text yesterday. That's why she left pissed off."

Ethan let out a whistle. "She has a right to be mad. But we don't have time to fix that issue. You go to the prison. Send Cole the file. When you're done at the prison, let's meet at your house."

They all had their assignments. Ian hoped his trip to the federal penitentiary would give him the answers he needed.

* * *

Mr. Ainsworth sat across from Ian in the interrogation room. Tex had pulled strings to get a private room and no guards. Ian wouldn't leave until he had answers. Prison hadn't been good to Mr. Ainsworth. The sides of his head had been shaven, and he looked to have lost weight, and if that wasn't enough of a clue, the black eye was a clear indicator that he had an issue in prison. He had screwed over many high rollers with long reaches. Mr. Ainsworth wouldn't make it more than a few months before someone took his life.

"Who would go after Bella?" Ian asked.

"I've got many enemies."

The vague response made Ian's temper rise. He didn't have time to sit and play twenty questions. Ian leapt out of his chair and wrapped his hands around Mr. Ainsworth's throat. The man's hands were tied to the table, and he was unable to fight back. Ian gave an extra squeeze before he let go. The second Ian's hands lifted, Mr. Ainsworth gasped for breath.

Ian towered over him. "Tell me who has a private plane man and a wife younger than him and who would take Bella."

Mr. Ainsworth closed his eyes for a second. "My kids."

"I need to know why and where would they take her."

"I'll tell you what you want, but I want to be transferred."

"You'll be lucky to live if you don't tell me how to find her. Bella has been through shit because of you, and she worked her ass off."

Ian held his breath, not sure if he would get the answer he needed.

"They probably found out about the offshore accounts if they raided my bunker. The accounts are in Bella's name. My children would take her back to San Diego… I cooperated. Can you help me?"

Ian nodded and turned and left the room. If they found Bella in time, he would have Tex talk to the warden, but not before he made sure of Bella's safety. If he didn't make it to her in time, he would come back and kill Mr. Ainsworth himself.

As he walked to the car, he dialed Cole. "I need you to book me a flight to San Diego."

"No need. I have a plane standing by. Meet us at the airstrip."

Ian would owe Cole big-time. If he had a plane, it

belonged to his family, and Cole asking his family for something was a big deal.

His next call was to Wolf. They would need his help when they landed. Wolf was part of SEAL Team Six, stationed in San Diego.

CHAPTER 12

Bella's head felt as if a band of drummers used it as a drum. She took inventory of her body: legs bound, hands bound, and muscles aching from her prolonged position. Bella had no clue how long she had been out.

Her last memory was when she'd tried to escape from the trunk. Her kidnappers had taken her to an airfield. No one would find her or know of her disappearance until Monday. Bella hoped she would live long enough to see Monday. She didn't understand what her kidnappers were after.

A sudden thirst came over her. She slowly opened her eyes to see her surroundings. The couple who'd kidnapped her sat in the leather airplane chairs across from her. Their heads were lowered, and they were in a deep discussion. With her kidnappers preoccupied in an argument, Bella looked around the plane to see if there was anyone else.

The airplane hit an air pocket, which caused Bella to jerk. The sudden movement sent pain through her body, and she let out a groan before she could stop herself. She stilled and hoped the kidnappers thought she was still asleep, but it didn't work. She heard the heels of the woman click across the plane floor.

"We know you are awake, bitch."

Bella slowly pried her eyes open. After she passed out, they must have injected her with a sleep aid. Her head felt cloudy.

The woman had her arms crossed, and she tapped her foot. Bella tried to say something, but her mouth was dry, and her throat was scratchy. She finally choked out the word "Water." Nobody moved to get her any.

Finally, Ryan went to the cockpit and came back with a bottle of water. He opened it, and Bella immediately opened her mouth. Ryan only gave her enough to wet her mouth.

"Why did you kidnap me?

"Don't play *poor me*. We know you have our father's money."

She blinked a couple of times and focused on their faces. Why hadn't she seen it from the beginning? These were Mr. Ainsworth's kids. They thought she'd been in on his scam. "What money?"

"Dear old Dad moved the money from all of the accounts to an offshore account in your name. We want you to transfer the money back to us. It's ours, not yours."

Tina and Ryan were spoiled brats. They'd never worked a day in their lives. Bella bet that without Daddy's pipeline of money, they were about to run out of funds. But they'd come to the wrong person. Bella knew nothing about missing money. And if she'd had a bank account in the Cayman Islands, she would have turned the money over to the people Mr. Ainsworth had stolen from.

"Your dad didn't give me any money. I have no clue about offshore accounts."

With Bella's hands tied behind her back, she couldn't block the hit that came her way. The word *terrified* didn't begin to describe how she felt, being thirty thousand feet in the air with no clue where they were headed and knowing that two crazy spoiled kids wanted one thing from her, and when they got it, they would kill her. But she didn't have an answer to what their dad had done.

"We are taking you back to San Diego." The crazy lady paced the aisle of the plane. "We have a friend that can get any information we need out of someone. You will tell us how to access the accounts. We need that money." She reached up and wiped her nose. Someone had a cocaine habit. Bella could only imagine that Mr. Ainsworth's daughter had been doing cocaine and run out of money. She might have drug dealers knocking on the door, wanting money, and she wasn't able to pay them back. Each scenario wasn't good for Bella. And if they needed money so badly, why were they in a private plane?

"It doesn't look like you need money. This plane ride can't be cheap."

"Let's just say we have another party instr—"

When the crazy bitch elbowed Ryan in the gut, he groaned in pain. Bella could see the blood spread on his shirt from where she'd stabbed him. But she'd learned one thing before Tina had elbowed him: they owed money to a powerful person, and he'd funded her kidnapping. She really wished she knew why Mr. Ainsworth had put the money in her name and how she could retrieve the money. When she did, they would kill her anyway.

Ryan rubbed his side. "Why don't you sleep the rest of the way? I don't want to deal with you, and it seems you will not tell us what we want to know." He pulled out a needle from his jacket.

"No. I won't say a word."

Her plea fell on deaf ears. As the needle entered her neck, her eyelids got heavy. She worked to keep herself awake. She didn't want to fall asleep, but the drug took over and knocked her out.

* * *

Ian glanced around the Cole family private jet. He was grateful his friend had borrowed it. Cole and Ian could bring their guns along and not have to worry about TSA. Ethan and Max sat in a leather chairs across from him and Cole. Ian hadn't expected them to come to San Diego, but they'd showed up at the airfield.

They were halfway through the three-hour flight from San Antonio to San Diego. He wished the pilot would put the plane in hyper speed. Bella's kidnappers had an eight-hour head start. Ian had spoken with Matthew "Wolf" Steel when he left the prison. Wolf and a couple of men from his unit would meet him at the airport when he landed.

He already owed Wolf and his unit. They'd saved him from death in North Korea. It had been years since he'd spoken to Wolf. He wished they were meeting under better circumstances.

Ian could have sworn he heard a phone ring. Seconds later, the flight attendant walked out with a satellite phone. "Mr. Parker, you have a call."

Ian clicked the speakerphone button. "Hello."

"Ian, it's Tex. I've patched Wolf in on the call. Wolf and I wanted to strategize while you were in the air so when you landed, we could hit the ground running."

Ian was amazed with Tex. How had he managed to get the phone number to the sat phone on the plane? But he didn't want Wolf and his men to get in trouble. This wasn't a government-sanctioned mission. They could put their lives and careers in jeopardy if they helped.

"Wolf… I appreciate everything. I called you when my emotions were high and desperate. I can't have you risk getting in trouble."

A growl came through the phone. "You are not forcing me to do anything. Answer one question: Do you love her?"

Ian had only started to see Bella in the last few weeks. Was what he felt love? Could a person fall that fast for someone? He didn't care if others thought he'd fallen too fast. "Yes, I love her. I know it hasn't been long, but I just know."

"You don't have to explain that to me. I fell for Caroline the second she sat down next to me on that stupid commercial flight where we both almost died because someone tried to hijack the plane. It might've been one of the worst and best flights of my life. Caroline is my everything. I know you wouldn't have called unless you felt the same way. We will help you get your woman back."

Ian's throat tightened with emotion. He knew the story of how Wolf and Caroline had met. She'd saved him when the ice in the drink didn't smell right.

Tex cut in. "Now that we have that out of the way, Ryan and Tina—Mr. Ainsworth's only kids—need money. Tina has a cocaine habit of a hundred thousand dollars a month."

Cole let out a whistle.

Tex continued. "Ryan's nose is clean, but he has a huge gambling problem. He owes money to the Mafia. According to financials, they are out of money, but someone funded their trip to San Antonio. It's either the Italian mob or the Mexican drug cartel. Either way, it doesn't look good."

"So they needed Bella to retrieve the money? But when you moved it, did we put her in further danger?"

Ian had to get Bella before they turned her over to the Mafia or the cartel. *Fuck.* It could be both groups. Tex had pulled the offshore-account information earlier and discovered that it contained thirty million dollars. Tex's magical program had transferred the money out of the account and into a shell company. Once Bella was safe, they would let the authorities know about the money.

"I made it look like the money was still there. I also pinpointed the house where they're holding her in San Diego."

The next hour would go by slowly. Ian wanted to bust the door down and go rescue Bella, guns blazing.

"What's the address?"

Tex let out a sigh. "You aren't a lone ranger. Wolf sent Benny and Dude to the house. They are set up to watch the perimeter. I have satellite setup on the house. These people aren't messing around. I counted five armed guards around the house. We need to wait until dark so we'll have extra cover."

"What if they kill her?"

Wolf's voice came through the phone. "I've read

the report on your woman. She's strong. Now, get your ass to San Diego so we can save her and have a beer. I'll meet you at the airport, and we'll gear up."

Wolf and Tex clicked off the phone. Ian closed his eyes and sent a prayer. He didn't know what he would do if he lost Bella. Hell, he'd just figured out he loved her, and he might lose her already. When he got her back, she would never leave his side again.

Cole leaned back in his chair. "Your woman sure knows how to get caught in a mess."

"It's not her fault," Ian growled. How could she have known that her crazy boss had set her up?

Cole held up his hands. "I didn't mean it in a bad way, but fuck, her boss screwed her over. Her first flip, she gets a crazy ex-homeowner, and now she's kidnapped and handed over to the Mafia."

Ian knew that what his friend had said was true. His nerves were on edge, and all he wanted was to wrap his arms around Bella.

CHAPTER 13

Ian watched the mansion through a pair of binoculars. He sat in a white van with Wolf, Dude, and Cole. Faulkner "Dude" Cooper was a member of Wolf's team. Dude was always in control and was the team's explosives expert. Ian hoped they wouldn't need Dude's expertise that night.

Abe and Cookie, two more members of Wolf's team, joined Max and Ethan in the SUV parked across the street. Abe had gotten his name because he was always honest. All SEALs could swim well, but Cookie could out swim anyone on the team. Ian felt comfortable working with Wolf's team. Cole and Ian had worked with them a few times before the North Koreans had captured them.

The clock struck ten. It was time to go. Ian

opened his door. Abe and Cookie jumped out of the SUV.

"Let's get my woman back," he growled to the surrounding men.

"Hooyah," they answered.

Ian lowered his night-vision goggles. Wolf's voice came over the comm. Ian gripped his gun in his right hand and nodded. Abe and Cookie headed around to the back of the house. Ethan and Max stayed in the vehicle and watched surveillance. Wolf and Cole flanked Ian.

Tex had been able to get a blueprint of the house. They figured the kidnappers held her in the back-right side of the building. The room had no windows and no way to escape. It would be the best room for holding a prisoner.

Cookie's voice came over the comm. "Two tangos down."

Ian stood behind the third tango and wrapped his arm around the man's throat. After a few seconds, the man dropped. Cole worked to tie his hands and feet together. Ian tied a cloth around his mouth. Their goal was to get Bella back, not kill members of organized crime.

Wolf took the last tango down with a punch. The

enemy never saw it coming. Wolf moved with the speed of light.

"All tangos have been cleared," Tex said over the comm. He was watching from a satellite.

The front door was locked. Abe and Cookie were in place at the back of the house. They waited for Ian's cue to enter. Ian worked a camera under the seal of the door. The four-inch monitor in his hands lit up with a picture of the entryway. He used the joystick attached to the monitor to view the rest of the area. Nobody stood guard behind the door. Ian stepped back and put the camera in his backpack, and Cole used his toolkit to unlock the door.

Once inside, Ian worked his way left, followed by Cole and Wolf. Abe and Cookie entered at the back and headed upstairs to clear the area. Ian could hear voices toward the back of the house.

When he and Cole reached the door to the room with no windows, Ian could hear someone speaking. He leaned close to the door to listen. He didn't want to go in unprepared, but when a gunshot sounded inside the room, he didn't wait any longer. He busted through the door. Wolf tried to stop him, but Ian was already on his way into the room. Bella was his first concern.

* * *

Bella felt drained from the numerous injections she had received. Ryan kept asking the same question, "What is the password?" She hadn't known the password ten minutes before. Why would she know it now? And even if she did know it, she wouldn't tell those two spoiled brats.

Then Bella spotted a scary man dressed in a thousand-dollar suit. He was sitting in a tall-back chair. If she hadn't seen him, the stench of his cigar would have given him away.

The man hadn't said a word to her. He answered a phone call and spoke in perfect Italian. She was screwed. Not only did her ex-boss's kids want something from her, but she also had the fucking mob after her. The situation kept getting worse. She didn't even know what day it was or how long she'd been out. The damn drugs they'd pumped into her system had messed with her sense of time.

"Why don't you ask your dad how to access the accounts? I'm telling you, I have nothing to do with them," Bella pleaded.

Tina tapped her manicured hand on the wood desk. "How do you expect us to ask our father when he is in jail and they monitor his calls, you dumb bitch?"

Bella didn't see the hand coming until it was too late. Ryan had attached her hands to the chair, and he'd also tied her feet together. There was no way she could have dodged the blow even if she'd tried. Tina's hand hit Bella's face with so much force that it made blood trickle from her nose. Luckily, the drugs still coursed through her body, and she felt numb. The first hit didn't hurt too badly, but when Tina came down with the second hit, Bella felt it to the core. Her head bobbed to the side, and black crept into her eyes.

She took a few calm breaths to get her emotions in check. Her vision came back. When she looked up, Tina's arm was in a downward trajectory again. Bella squeezed her eyes and waited for impact, but it didn't come. She opened her eyes to see the scary man in the expensive suit. He had Tina's arm in his hand. He'd already looked intimidating when he was in the chair. Now he oozed danger as his six-foot-five frame stood in front of her. The perfectly tailored suit accented his well-defined body. If Bella hadn't already fallen in love with an ex-Navy SEAL house-flipping sex god, she might have gone for the angry, dangerous mob lord—though she didn't know how she would make it in the crime family.

If she hadn't already figured out that the man was part of the Mafia, it became obvious when he spoke. "Go sit, Tina." His heavy Italian accent made it hard to understand him.

"Sir, please let me go. I don't know what they told you, but I don't know where any money is. Their father screwed me over like he scr—"

"Shut up." He lowered himself in front of her. "My tech guys say the password is your childhood animal's name. Now, tell me the name." He reached out and held her hand. His touch sent goose bumps through her body—and not the good kind. They formed out of pure terror of the man in front of her.

Bella took a second to figure out how to answer. Would Mr. Ainsworth really use her childhood pet's name? She couldn't chance it. If she told them the name, they would get what they wanted and kill her. If she continued to stall, someone might show up and save her. The likelihood of anyone knowing her location was slim. She hadn't left Ian on good terms. He probably wanted nothing to do with her after she stormed out and didn't give him a chance.

It was too bad. As Bella stared death in the face, she wished she'd told Ian she loved him, even if it was too early for that. You never knew when you might die. Now she wouldn't be able to tell the only man she'd ever loved how she felt. But one thing was for sure: she wouldn't tell these fuckers her childhood pet's name.

"Buffy."

Scary Italian guy stared into her eyes. He cocked his head to the side. "Lie." Before she had a chance to figure out his next move, he pulled her finger back until it snapped. The pain that jolted through her body was enough to make her scream bloody murder. The fucker had broken her finger with a flick of his hand. He hadn't even flinched.

"Put something in her mouth. I don't need to listen to her scream."

Ryan looked around the room until he found a handkerchief and shoved it in her mouth. He had to try a couple of times because his hands shook. He seemed as shocked as she was by the crazy fucker's action. Tina didn't look surprised. She looked down at her manicured nails and ignored the incident in front of her.

Tears streamed down Bella's face. A sob broke from her, but the towel muffled her screams.

"Now, let's try this again. What is your childhood pet's name?"

Bella didn't know what to do. How had the man in front of her known she was lying? Was that a test before he asked the real question? She didn't know how much torture she could take, but she couldn't give in.

"Mol—" Bella didn't even get the full word out before he grabbed her middle finger and pushed it back as far as it could go. The pain so intense that her world went dark.

They put smelling salts under her nose, and she woke up and wanted to vomit from the smell. They kept the handkerchief in her mouth. The tears in her eyes made it hard to see, and the handkerchief made it hard to breathe. Blood and snot streamed from her nose.

"Last time. What is your pet's name?" The crazy Italian removed the handkerchief from her mouth.

Bella felt defeated. "Scarlett."

He nodded, reached for her first dislocated finger, and snapped it into place. Bella let out a scream, and before she knew what he was doing, he'd snapped her second finger back into place. The pain was as bad as when he'd dislocated them—maybe even worse.

Ryan looked as if he wanted to vomit. Bella didn't blame him. If she had to watch a crazy person torture someone, she would look green too. An idea formed in her mind. If she could get him alone, she might have a chance to get away. He didn't look happy with the way his sister and the crazy Italian were treating her.

"Water," Bella croaked out. *This will get one person out of the room.*

The crazy guy looked at Tina. "Go get her water."

Tina rolled her eyes and exited to the right. *Fuck.* The room had an attached bathroom. Bella couldn't get a break.

Ryan took a few steps in Bella's direction. "Don't you think this is a little overboard?"

The crazy Italian took his attention away from Bella. "Do you have money to pay for your sister's drug habit? Tina promised me fifty percent of the money in the account if I could get the info from her."

"Hey, man, that's my money too, and I promised nothing like that."

Tina walked out of the bathroom, raised her gun, and pressed the trigger. She shot her brother without even blinking. For the first time, Bella saw shock in the crazy Italian's eyes. He hadn't expected her to take out her own brother.

Bella hadn't had time to contemplate what

happened when the doors of the study burst open. She had to blink the tears away to see who came through. She couldn't believe her eyes—her knight in shining armor had arrived. He'd come for her even though she'd thrown a fit the day before and hadn't listened to a word he'd said.

Danger still loomed around them. Bella's heart leaped. She didn't want Ian or his friends to get hurt. Tina raised her gun to shoot Ian, and Bella screamed. She heard two shots. Ian jumped to the side and dodged a bullet. Tina's body slumped to the ground.

The crazy Italian raised his gun but stopped when one of Ian's men shoved a gun in his back. "Pull that trigger, and you will die."

When the Italian dropped his gun, Ian's friend put his hands in zip ties.

Ian rushed to Bella's side and worked on her bindings. "I'm so sorry. Please forgive me."

Silly man. She'd forgiven him hours before, and he had bonus points because he'd come to her rescue.

He ran a cold rag over her face and wiped the blood away. After making sure she was somewhat okay, he gave his attention to his friends. "Wolf, you and your team need to leave. I'm going to call the paramedics." When it looked as though they would protest, Ian said, "Man, it will be a pain in the butt to explain you and your team. Cole and I came after my girlfriend." He got up and gave each man a one-armed hug, and they disappeared in a flash. Bella hoped she would get to meet the people who'd helped save her life. There was no mistaking that she would have died if it weren't for Ian and his friends.

Ian had his work cut out explaining to the cops how he and one other guy had taken down five guards and rescued Bella. But the crazy Italian had been on the cops' radar for months. Their search warrants had been turned down. They finally had something to bring him in on, and they were happy to believe Ian's story in the end.

CHAPTER 14

Two weeks had passed since Bella had been kidnapped and taken across the country. She was happy to be back in Texas, though every sound still made her jump, and the splint on her hand annoyed her. The doctor said she could remove it in another week. The swelling had gone down, and in its place, her hand turned black and blue.

Ava's heels clicked across the hardwood floor. She wrapped Bella in a hug and handed her a glass of wine. "Congrats. We sold it for ten thousand over asking, and all cash. Ten-day closing, and you can start your next flip."

Excitement coursed through Bella's veins. She had sat down with Cole and Ian and decided to go into business with them. This last flip had almost been the death of her. First, Jake would have killed her if Ian hadn't shown up when he had. Then she'd had to deal with the crazy brother and sister.

Tina had survived the gunshot and was serving time for attempted murder. The Italian, Vezio Astor, was the head of the Astor crime family. She hadn't recognized him at the house, but later, when they said his name, she knew who he was. The FBI had tried to arrest Vezio many times, but he had a high-ranking judge in his pocket.

Vezio wouldn't be able to escape prison this time. Because he'd used his house to kidnap and hold Bella against her will, the FBI was able to search the house, and they'd found documentation of his drug deals.

Tex had turned over all the information on the offshore accounts to the FBI. They were able to funnel money back to families, and the FBI had increased Mr. Ainsworth's sentence. Bella no longer had to deal with her past. In the back of her mind, she felt bad for Ryan. He'd been an ass to kidnap her, but she'd never wanted anyone to die.

Ava handed her the contract.

"It doesn't seem real yet." Bella couldn't believe the house was sold.

Ava leaned against the gray wall. "You did an

amazing job with this house. It was one of the easiest sales I've had. But next time, don't open the door for anyone trying to buy the house. I'll let you know if someone is coming. I thought we'd lost you, Bella." Tears formed in Ava's eyes.

Bella's eyes started to tear up as well. She sniffled. "I didn't mean to get kidnapped."

Ava laughed. "I don't think most people try to get kidnapped. I'm happy you're going to start to work with Ian and Cole on your next projects. You both should come over next weekend, and have Cole come too. I think we need to set him up with someone."

"I'll ask Ian." Bella leaned in and was about to give her friend a hug goodbye when a knock on the front door made her heart rate skyrocket. She still was afraid when people came to the door. Ian hadn't left her side until that day, when he'd gone to the courthouse with Cole to purchase their next flip.

As soon as she was done with Ava, Bella wanted to head over to the house that Ian and Cole planned to purchase at the auction that day. She pulled from Ava's embrace, walked toward the door, and gripped the pink switchblade Ian had given her when they got back to Texas. She opened the door.

Ian stood on the steps with a bouquet. He swept

her into a hug. "Congratulations. I wanted to bring you flowers."

Ava slid by her on the way out the door and gave her a thumbs-up.

"Why aren't you with Cole?" she asked. "Did we not get the house?"

Ian captured her lips with a kiss. She was so lost in his touch that she forgot all about her questions until he pulled back with a smirk on his face. "Of course we got the house. Cole went over to check it out. You and I are heading west to spend the next ten days in a cabin on the river."

Bella liked the idea of getting away.

* * *

Ian couldn't wait to strip Bella down the second they walked through the doors of the cabin. She squeaked when he picked her up and pressed her back against the wall. During the two-hour drive, he'd watched her dress ride up her legs.

She immediately wrapped her legs around his waist and clawed at his belt. He guided her dress over her head. The second he had her stripped down, he pressed his lips to hers. Pure need coursed through his body. Ever since she'd been taken from him, he constantly needed her touch.

"You need to move in with me," Ian said between kisses.

Bella's hooded eyes opened. "Last time I checked, you are supposed to ask the woman to move in with you, not demand it."

"I don't want there to be a chance for you to say no." Ian ran his hands through her velvety folds. She was ready for him. He couldn't hold back any longer. Ian pushed into her hard and fast. The need to possess her was overwhelming.

Bella threw her head back against the door and let out a moan. Her channel clenched against his dick, causing him to move faster. She grabbed his hair and pulled him in. The kiss was raw and full of passion.

When he reached between them and pinched her nub, Bella screamed his name, and he felt her tighten around him. Ian couldn't hold on much longer. He gripped her ass with both hands and thrust into her. With one final thrust, he came. They were both panting from the intense passion. Ian leaned his head against her. He didn't want to pull out and lose the connection.

"Yes," she whispered.

"You'll move in with me?" Ian wanted to come home every night and have Bella in his arms. He knew it was too early to ask her to marry him, but if it were up to him, he would take her to the courthouse right then and make her his.

"I want a ring one day."

Ian stopped stroking her back. He walked over to the couch with Bella in his arms. The cabin out in the woods would be the perfect way to spend the weekend. Bella agreed to live with him, and she wanted a ring.

Ian dragged his hands along the curve of her breast. "You will be my wife one day, Bella. I didn't want to ask this soon and scare you off."

"When you're ready to ask, I'll say yes."

"Good. So you'll move in when we get back." He kissed her on the forehead. "And shortly, I will ask you to marry me."

Ian wouldn't wait long to ask Bella to marry him. A plan started to formulate in his mind. Bella had been upset that she hadn't gotten to meet Wolf and his team. They'd vacated Vezio's house before Ian had called the cops. Cole and Ian would have loved to stay in San Diego for a few more days, but the longer Cole kept the plane, the more he would owe his family. If Cole hadn't gotten the jet to take them to San Diego, they wouldn't have made it in time, and Bella would be dead. Ian vowed to help Cole with any favor his family demanded.

In a couple of months, Ian planned to take Bella back to San Diego so she could meet the men who'd helped save her. He also planned to make her his wife on the beach.

"Bella, I love you."

Tears formed in Bella's eyes, and Ian panicked that he said something wrong.

"I love you too, Ian," Bella whispered.

Ian wiped the tear from her cheeks. "Why are you crying?"

"I'm happy."

"Me too, love."

EPILOGUE

Cole Walker reached for his phone in his front pocket. They wouldn't stop the calls until he answered. When he'd promised to do anything his family wanted, he'd been in a panic because he hadn't wanted anything to happen to Bella.

He'd known they would call, but he hadn't thought it would be only two weeks after he'd called his eldest brother and asked to use the plane. That was the first time in eight years that he'd heard his brother's voice. Bryson had said he could use the plane, but he'd owe his brother a favor. Nothing in the Walker family came for free.

Bryson ran Walker Oil. Cole assumed his brother wasn't doing things aboveboard. Ian sure as hell knew his father was corrupt. The second he heard

Cole's father had taken money to shut down a school program, he'd lost all respect for him.

Cole's mom had turned a blind eye to his father's dealings. As long as she kept the lifestyle she was used to, she didn't care what he did. Cole hadn't even thought of her as his mom when he was growing up. He was raised by nannies. His mom couldn't be bothered to take care of her kids. Nathen, his other brother, had become sick when his parents were overseas, and his mom wouldn't cut the trip short, so Nathen spent six days in ICU without his mom. Cole never understood how his two older brothers had stayed around to deal with his parents.

Bryson seemed to be calling in his favor. It had been the fifth time he called in the past five hours. He'd left voicemails, but Cole had chosen not to listen to them. Cole guessed it was time to pay up.

He leaned back in his Range Rover and looked at the house he'd just purchased. He wanted to look inside and give Ian and Bella an update. They'd purchased the house sight unseen. The price was lower than the lot, so if all failed, they would tear the house down.

Bryson's name flashed across the screen. Cole

swiped his finger to get the conversation over with and see what he'd sold his soul for. "Bryson."

"About time you fucking answered. You need to answer when I call." Bryson expected everyone to jump when he spoke. It was one of the reasons they didn't get along.

Cole pinched the bridge of his nose and took a few calming breaths. "What do you need, Bryson?"

"You are to be at family dinner this Sunday."

Attending a family dinner wasn't what he'd expected Bryson would demand. Cole hadn't talked to anyone in his family in eight years, including his parents. He didn't want to see any of them.

"Is this the favor? If I show up to family dinner, you won't ask me to do anything else?"

"No, we will discuss your favor after family dinner. Be at Mom and Dad's Sunday at seven."

Before Cole had time to respond, Bryson clicked the phone off. *Fuck.* One dinner. He could do this.

He had six days to figure out what to do with his family. Cole walked up to the condemned house they'd just purchased at auction. When he opened the door, he was hit with a smell so strong he thought he would throw up. It smelled like a mixture of crap and vomit.

Using his shirt, he covered his nose and headed

into the house. Poop was smeared over the walls in the living room. Trash lined the floor, and he had to step over a pile of needles. The house seemed to be a crack den. He reached for his gun in his holster. Cole never left his house without his Glock.

Each room he walked through was lined with trash and human fecal matter. He couldn't understand how someone could squat in that house. When he entered the last room, he stopped in his tracks. A woman who was skin and bones and covered in dirt was pointing a gun at him.

"Ma'am, please lower the gun, and we can talk."

"You won't take me back."

He didn't have time to ask questions before she fired the gun in his direction.

The End

Cole's story is coming in 2019. Make sure to sign up for my newsletter so you don't miss a New Release.

Join Linzi Baxter Newsletter at Newsletter

AUTHOR'S NOTE

White Hat Security Series

Hacker Exposed

Royal Hacker

Misunderstood Hacker

Undercover Hacker

Hacker Revelation

Hacker Christmans (Dec 2018)

Montana Gold (Brotherhood Kindle World)

Grayson's Angel

Noah - Nov 2018

A Flipping Love Story (Badge of Honor World)

Unlocking Dreams
Unlocking Hope - 2019

Visit linzibaxter.com for more information and release dates.

Join Linzi Baxter Newsletter at Newsletter

GRAYSON'S ANGEL
MONTANA GOLD

A life she thought she left behind...

Kara Davidson left Montana years ago. After her mother died, she decided to never step foot in the state again. Then she gets a call saying her father is in the hospital. Her trip home is supposed to be quick. She didn't count on meeting a retired Navy SEAL who made her body come alive.

A retired Navy SEAL looking forward to vacation...

Grayson Steele was looking forward to a vacation with old friends. The vacation starts out perfect when he is seated next to a blond angel on the flight to Montana. He didn't expect to see her again or for her to jump into his car wearing a bloody wedding dress.

Will Grayson be able to help Kara untangle the lies of her past before it's too late? Or will an unexpected enemy take Kara from Grayson?

HACKER EXPOSED

WHITE HAT SECURITY, BOOK 1

BUY NOW

After my father loses the Ross fortune in a pyramid scheme, I never expect to see Alex and his brothers again. But fate has other plans.

It's been ten years since my family went into hiding, ten years since I last saw the chiseled face of Alex. But he haunts my dreams, like a ghost who won't leave me alone. Now a hacker in charge of a cybersecurity agency, I refuse to visit my father while he's rotting away in prison. In fact, I want nothing more than to forget the whole thing happened at all.

But the minute Alex Ross walks back into my life, ignoring my past becomes impossible. A million dollars has been stolen from his company, and he needs my help to track down the culprit. I don't need the distraction, but with a body carved from marble and a face that would make even da Vinci weep, Alex is just that. I should say no...

Instead, driven by a desperate need to redeem myself and my family, I reluctantly agree. But as I dig deeper into the theft from Ross Enterprise, and the thief goes to incredible lengths to evade the police, we find ourselves caught in the crossfire.

ABOUT AUTHOR

Linzi Baxter lives in Orlando, Florida with her husband and lazy basset hound. She started writing when voices inside her head wouldn't stop talking until the story was told. When not at work as an IT Manager, Linzi enjoys writing action-packed romances that will take you to the edge of your seat.

She enjoys engaging her readers with strong, interesting characters that have complex and stimulating stories to tell. If you enjoy a little (or maybe a whole lot) of steam and spice, don't miss checking out White Hat Security series.

When not writing, Linzi enjoys reading, watching college sports (GO UCF Knights), and traveling to Europe. She loves hearing from her readers and can't wait to hear from you!

There are many more books in this fan fiction world than listed here, for an up-to-date list go to www.AcesPress.com

You can also visit our Amazon page at: http://www.amazon.com/author/operationalpha

Special Forces: Operation Alpha World

Denise Agnew: Dangerous to Hold
Shauna Allen: Awakening Aubrey
Shauna Allen: Defending Danielle
Shauna Allen: Rescuing Rebekah
Shauna Allen: Saving Scarlett
Shauna Allen: Saving Grace
Brynne Asher: Blackburn
Jennifer Becker: Hiding Catherine
Julia Bright: Saving Lorelei
Julia Bright: Rescuing Amy
Victoria Bright: Surviving Savage
Victoria Bright: Going Ghost
Victoria Bright: Jostling Joker
Cara Carnes: Protecting Mari
Kendra Mei Chailyn: Beast
Kendra Mei Chailyn: Barbie
Kendra Mei Chailyn : Pitbull

Melissa Kay Clarke: Rescuing Annabeth
Melissa Kay Clarke: Safeguarding Miley
Samantha A. Cole: Handling Haven
Samantha A. Cole: Cheating the Devil
Sue Coletta: Hacked
Melissa Combs: Gallant
KaLyn Cooper: Rescuing Melina
Liz Crowe: Marking Mariah
Jordan Dane: Redemption for Avery
Jordan Dane: Fiona's Salvation
Riley Edwards: Protecting Olivia
Riley Edwards: Redeeming Violet
Riley Edwards, Recovering Ivy
Nicole Flockton: Protecting Maria
Nicole Flockton: Guarding Erin
Nicole Flockton: Guarding Suzie
Nicole Flockton: Guarding Brielle
Casey Hagen: Shielding Nebraska
Casey Hagen: Shielding Harlow
Casey Hagen: Shielding Josie
Casey Hagen: Shielding Blair
Desiree Holt: Protecting Maddie
Kathy Ivan: Saving Sarah
Kathy Ivan: Saving Savannah
Kathy Ivan: Saving Stephanie

Jesse Jacobson: Protecting Honor
Jesse Jacobson: Fighting for Honor
Jesse Jacobson: Defending Honor
Jesse Jacobson: Summer Breeze
Silver James: Rescue Moon
Silver James: SEAL Moon
Silver James: Assassin's Moon
Silver James: Under the Assassin's Moon
Becca Jameson: Saving Sofia
Kate Kinsley: Protecting Ava
Heather Long: Securing Arizona
Heather Long: Guarding Gertrude
Heather Long: Protecting Pilar
Heather Long: Covering Coco
Gennita Low: No Protection
Kirsten Lynn: Joining Forces for Jesse
Margaret Madigan: Bang for the Buck
Margaret Madigan: Buck the System
Margaret Madigan: Jungle Buck
Margaret Madigan: December Chill
Rachel McNeely: The SEAL's Surprise Baby
Rachel McNeely: The SEAL's Surprise Bride
Rachel McNeely: The SEAL's Surprise Twin
KD Michaels: Saving Laura
KD Michaels: Protecting Shane

KD Michaels: Avenging Angels
Wren Michaels: The Fox & The Hound
Wren Michaels: The Fox & The Hound 2
Wren Michaels: Shadow of Doubt
Wren Michaels: Shift of Fate
Wren Michaels: Steeling His Heart
Kat Mizera: Protecting Bobbi
Mary B Moore: Force Protection
LeTeisha Newton: Protecting Butterfly
LeTeisha Newton: Protecting Goddess
LeTeisha Newton: Protecting Vixen
LeTeisha Newton: Protecting Heartbeat
MJ Nightingale: Protecting Beauty
MJ Nightingale: Betting on Benny
MJ Nightingale: Protecting Secrets
Sarah O'Rourke: Saving Liberty
Debra Parmley: Protecting Pippa
Lainey Reese: Protecting New York
Jenika Snow: Protecting Lily
Jen Talty: Burning Desire
Jen Talty: Burning Kiss
Jen Talty: Burning Skies
Jen Talty: Burning Lies
Jen Talty: Burning Heart
Megan Vernon: Protecting Us
Megan Vernon: Protecting Earth

Fire and Police: Operation Alpha World

KaLyn Cooper: Justice for Gwen

Aspen Drake: Sheltering Emma

As you know, this book included at least one character from Susan Stoker's books. To check out more, see below.

Delta Force Heroes Series

Rescuing Rayne (FREE!)
Rescuing Aimee (novella)
Rescuing Emily
Rescuing Harley
Marrying Emily
Rescuing Kassie
Rescuing Bryn
Rescuing Casey
Rescuing Sadie
Rescuing Wendy
Rescuing Mary (Oct 2018)
Rescuing Macie (April 2019)

Badge of Honor: Texas Heroes Series

Justice for Mackenzie (FREE!)
Justice for Mickie
Justice for Corrie
Justice for Laine (novella)
Shelter for Elizabeth
Justice for Boone

Shelter for Adeline

Shelter for Sophie

Justice for Erin

Justice for Milena

Shelter for Blythe

Justice for Hope

Shelter for Quinn (Feb 2019)

Shelter for Koren (June 2019)

Shelter for Penelope (Oct 2019)

SEAL of Protection Series

Protecting Caroline (FREE!)

Protecting Alabama

Protecting Fiona

Marrying Caroline (novella)

Protecting Summer

Protecting Cheyenne

Protecting Jessyka

Protecting Julie (novella)

Protecting Melody

Protecting the Future

Protecting Kiera (novella)

Protecting Dakota

SEAL of Protection: Legacy Series

Securing Caite (Jan 2019)

Securing Sidney (May 2019)
Securing Piper (Sept 2019)
Securing Zoey (TBA)
Securing Avery (TBA)
Securing Kalee (TBA)

New York Times, USA Today and *Wall Street Journal* Bestselling Author Susan Stoker has a heart as big as the state of Texas where she lives, but this all American girl has also spent the last fourteen years living in Missouri, California, Colorado, and Indiana. She's married to a retired Army man who now gets to follow *her* around the country.

She debuted her first series in 2014 and quickly followed that up with the SEAL of Protection Series, which solidified her love of writing and creating stories readers can get lost in.

If you enjoyed this book, or any book, please consider leaving a review. It's appreciated by authors more than you'll know.

www.stokeraces.com
www.AcesPress.com
susan@stokeraces.com

Made in the USA
Middletown, DE
30 December 2019

82254569R00096